"Emily deserves a mommy," Ronnie said

"The less of your time I take up, the sooner you'll find the right woman. For both of you."

The idea of Jason with any other woman sent a pang through her so sharp she almost doubled over.

Jason looked at her with a sad smile. "So I guess tonight is pretty much it, then?"

Pretty much. But she couldn't force herself to agree with him. "Does tonight have to be over already?"

His eyes were unreadable in the dark. "I don't want to take advantage....You don't owe me anything."

Her laugh was strangled. "I want this for *me*. I want you." She had since the first day they'd met and he'd smiled at her, his blue eyes shadowed with hurts she'd wanted to kiss away.

Dear Reader,

In 2007 I made my Harlequin American Romance debut with *Trouble in Tennessee,* and in the very gracious fan mail I've received, readers consistently ask: Will Ronnie, the female mechanic with overbearing brothers, get her own book? Here it is!

With *An Unlikely Mommy,* I invite you to return (or make your first trip) to the small town of Joyous, Tennessee, and share Ronnie's story.

Veronica Carter lost her own mother at a young age and grew up among three brothers, eventually taking a job at her father's garage. She's a lousy cook, doesn't own a dress and doesn't have any maternal urges—at least, none that can't be satisfied by "borrowing" her niece for the day and returning her safely home later. But when Ronnie falls for Jason McDeere, single father to an adorable toddler daughter, she's forced to reevaluate what she thought she wanted and how she views herself. Is she really long-term Mommy material or is a relationship with Jason doomed to failure, compounding the hurt he and his daughter have already suffered?

Ronnie and Jason mean a lot to me, but I also had great fun with some of the secondary characters. Visit my Web site, www.tanyamichaels.com, for some of the "deleted scenes" between Lola Ann and Dev. And, of course, feel free to e-mail me at t.michaels@earthlink.net—I love to hear from readers!

Best wishes,

Tanya

An Unlikely Mommy
TANYA MICHAELS

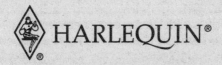

HARLEQUIN®

TORONTO • NEW YORK • LONDON
AMSTERDAM • PARIS • SYDNEY • HAMBURG
STOCKHOLM • ATHENS • TOKYO • MILAN • MADRID
PRAGUE • WARSAW • BUDAPEST • AUCKLAND

ISBN-13: 978-0-373-75207-2
ISBN-10:   0-373-75207-5

AN UNLIKELY MOMMY

www.eHarlequin.com

Printed in U.S.A.

ABOUT THE AUTHOR

Tanya Michaels started telling stories almost as soon as she could talk...and started stealing her mom's Harlequin romances less than a decade later. In 2003 Tanya was thrilled to have her first book, a romantic comedy, published by Harlequin Books. Since then, Tanya's sold nearly twenty books and is a two-time recipient of a Booksellers' Best Award as well as a finalist for the Holt Medallion, National Readers' Choice Award and Romance Writers of America's prestigious RITA® Award. Tanya lives in Georgia with her husband, two preschoolers and an unpredictable cat, but you can visit Tanya online at www.tanyamichaels.com.

Books by Tanya Michaels

HARLEQUIN AMERICAN ROMANCE
1170—TROUBLE IN TENNESSEE

HARLEQUIN TEMPTATION
968—HERS FOR THE WEEKEND
986—SHEER DECADENCE
1008—GOING ALL THE WAY

HARLEQUIN NEXT
DATING THE MRS. SMITHS
THE GOOD KIND OF CRAZY
MOTHERHOOD WITHOUT PAROLE

This is my fifteenth book to be released by Harlequin Books, and I can't imagine having hit this milestone without the encouragement, advice and friendship of the wonderful ladies (and men!) of Georgia Romance Writers. Thank you for all you've taught me and all you've seen me through.

Chapter One

"Did Webster's change the definition of *celebrate* and no one told me? Because I always thought it should involve being, you know, *happy*."

Veronica Carter turned her attention from the dance floor, with its multicolored spotlights and twirling couples, to Lola Ann Whitford, town librarian and Ronnie's best friend. While it was impossible to discern Lola Ann's every word over top of the exuberant local band that played every Friday night, the gist was clear.

"Sorry," Ronnie said sheepishly. "I'm not being very good company, am I?"

"No." The short, curvy brunette grinned, showing all her dimples. "Which is why I am ditching you for the very first guy who asks me to dance."

"Well, as long as he's hot," Ronnie conceded. After today's inspection of her new home, she *should* be feeling celebratory. Yet her emotions were as badly tangled as a carelessly handled fishing line.

In addition to the inspector telling her she'd chosen her future house well, and that the flaws were mostly cosmetic and the foundation was solid, she could still hear Wayne

Carter's resigned sigh. Her dad's eyes, the exact green as hers, had brimmed with wistful loss instead of eager joy, an image reversed in reflection. *I am twenty-five, more than old enough to move out.* She shouldn't feel guilty, like some ungrateful teenager running away to the big city in the middle of the night. Heck, Ronnie wouldn't even be changing zip codes.

Lola Ann snapped her fingers in front of Ronnie's face. "I've lost you again."

"No, I'm here. You're right about celebrating! Is it bad luck to toast the new place before it's legally mine?" In a few weeks, she'd officially close on the house…then spend the foreseeable future remodeling. Ronnie had always been mechanically inclined, better with power tools than curling irons or mascara wands, and without the quirks and superficial damages to the one-story brick home, she never would have been able to afford it. "Come on, I'm buying this round."

They edged their way through the dance hall's regular weekend crowd and stopped at the teak counter that ran parallel to the far left wall. Flannel-clad Jack Guthrie, his wire-rimmed glasses and silver hair taking on an otherworldly glow beneath the neon signs, had been the bartender here since time before memory. He'd poured Ronnie a drink the night she turned twenty-one and had done the same for her three brothers before her. He'd also served inaugural beers to her parents.

There was that pang again. Often she could think of her parents, the life they'd once shared, without missing her mother too terribly, but today—the approaching milestone of buying her first house—had left her nostalgic.

Forcing a smile, Ronnie placed a ten on the bar for two

drinks. In her peripheral vision, she saw that her oldest brother, Danny, was waiting to order. His wife, Kaitlyn, stood behind him, her face flushed with pleasure and the exertion of dancing. Children were allowed inside Guthrie Hall, and Ashley often accompanied her mother and father. Tonight, however, Ronnie's niece was hanging out with Grandpa Wayne, who'd promised to teach the second-grader how to play poker just as he'd taught Ronnie when she was around Ashley's age.

Ronnie caught her sister-in-law's eye, and Kaitlyn approached, nodding hello to Lola Ann.

"You look like you're having fun," Ronnie observed.

Kaitlyn bobbed her head in cheerful agreement. "I adore my daughter, but I need these occasional adults-only evenings to remind myself what a passionate, flirtatious man my husband can be."

Ronnie pretended to shudder. "I don't want to hear about passion and my brother in the same sentence."

"Fair enough." Kaitlyn chuckled. "Some unsolicited advice from an old married woman—when *you* get married, don't feel like you have to have kids right away. Take the time to savor those early newlywed years."

Sound, yet pointless, advice. Last time Ronnie had checked, dating was a prerequisite to marriage.

Men weren't exactly beating down her door—correction, her father's door—to ask Ronnie out. Her town identity as a skinny grease monkey had long been cemented. While even a flat-chested mechanic could attract male admirers once in a blue moon, her overprotective brothers had put an end to those few budding relationships, making marriage the least of Ronnie's current

concerns. Not that she minded being single. Once she
moved out of her dad's house, she selfishly planned to
make the most of the solitude—watching whatever *she*
wanted on the television set and not worrying about pre-
paring meals for anyone.

Danny joined them, handing his wife a cold bottle of
water and sipping draft beer from a plastic cup. With his
free hand, he tugged lightly on Ronnie's ponytail. "You
saving a dance for your big brother?"

"Nah, I'll leave you to a woman who can truly appreciate you." She jerked her chin toward Kaitlyn, then grinned
teasingly. "Personally, I'm holding out for a better offer."

Kaitlyn and Lola Ann both laughed at the jibe, but
Danny took the words at face value.

"Like who?" he asked, scanning the crowd with
narrowed eyes.

Ronnie groaned. "Kaitlyn, go keep your husband
occupied, won't you?"

"My pleasure." Ronnie's sister-in-law winked at them
and stood on tiptoe to whisper something in Danny's ear.
Giggling like teenagers, they headed toward a dimly lit
corner.

Turning back to Lola Ann, Ronnie sighed. "Does it
make me pathetic that the only invitation to dance I've had
since we got here is from my brother?"

Even if she weren't at a point in her life where she
yearned for his-and-her towel sets, the occasional two-
step partner would be nice. An image began to form in her
mind, of a man with light brown hair and storm-cloud-gray
eyes, but she shook off the ludicrous idea of being in his
arms. Beyond some chance encounters and casual hellos

Jason McDeere barely knew she existed. Besides, he almost never came to Guthrie's, much to the disappointment of the town's single women.

"You forget," Lola Ann said, "I'd *love* to be asked to dance by a Carter brother."

Sympathy tugged at Ronnie. A few months ago, she'd realized Lola Ann harbored a crush on Devin, the only remaining bachelor among Ronnie's siblings. Unfortunately, Dev seemed hell-bent on his bachelor status, having already dated half the eligible women in Joyous, Tennessee, and never staying with one for long.

"'Scuse me." A deep voice interrupted the women's conversation, and Ronnie looked up—and up—into the gentle brown eyes of Teddy Blinn. The nearly six-and-a-half-foot-tall man was known to most simply as Bear. "I hope I'm not interrupting you ladies?"

"Not at all." Ronnie craned her neck back as far as it would comfortably go and smiled hopefully. She'd danced with him once or twice before. While it was difficult to match his long-legged stride, he was at least big enough not to be intimidated by her brothers. "How are things with you?"

"Good, good. The truck's running great," he informed her. She'd ordered some engine parts for him last month. "You both look real pretty tonight."

With men like Bear, the compliment wasn't a come-on so much as part of the perfunctory courtesy his mama had instilled—like opening doors for others or saying "ma'am."

He edged a step closer to Lola Ann, their differences in height nearly comical. "I wondered if you'd do me the honor of a dance?"

"Love to." Lola Ann passed her drink to Ronnie. "Would you mind holding this?"

Some celebration, Ronnie thought with a wry smile. She'd been reduced to cup-holder in the absence of an unoccupied table.

Truthfully, she knew she wasn't scintillating company tonight, and she was glad to see Lola Ann having fun. Bear moved with surprising agility for a man his size, and the two of them seeming to be enjoying a brisk polka around the sawdust-sprinkled floor. When the song ended, Bear escorted Ronnie's friend back with the solicitousness of a boy who'd promised to have his date back by curfew.

Lola Ann fanned her face with her hand. "Whew. That was fun. Thanks, Bear."

"Always a pleasure." He touched the front of his gray cowboy hat. "Ronnie, maybe you and I can cut a rug later?"

"Sounds good." But as Bear walked away, she couldn't help a quick double check over her left shoulder.

Yep, there was her brother Devin, smiling noncommittally at something a blonde was saying, but keeping one eye on Ronnie. As a kid, she'd adopted tomboy mannerisms and hobbies, wanting to fit in with her three brothers so that she didn't get left behind while they camped or attended sporting events. Little had she known that all she had to do to get her brothers' attention was hold sixty seconds of conversation with anyone of—gasp!—the opposite sex. She crossed her eyes at Devin, watched him stifle a laugh, then turned away.

Unfortunately, Lola Ann had followed Ronnie's line of sight. The librarian scowled as fiercely as if she'd just caught someone defacing a reference book. "What has *she* got that I don't have? Besides mile-long legs, flowing gold hair and a size-two waist."

"You're every bit as pretty as she is," Ronnie insisted.

"Yet he's never asked me out. You'd think, with all the different women he dates, he'd have worked his way around to me eventually."

My fault. Lola Ann had probably been placed out of romantic bounds by virtue of being best friends with Devin's "kid sister." Not that Ronnie was a kid anymore, but Dev, who still called her Red and had given her pajamas featuring cartoon characters for her last birthday, obviously didn't think of her as an adult. Still, considering his track record, was it such a bad thing that he hadn't asked out Lola Ann? Ronnie would hate to see her friend hurt.

"Lola, you know I love him—he's my brother, so I'm obligated. But even I have to admit that he's…"

"Unable to emotionally connect? A commitment-phobe? A serial dater?" Lola Ann sighed. "You're right, of course. The problem is, I've spent too much time with your family and got to know him as a real human being."

In a way that most of his dates probably hadn't, Ronnie acknowledged silently. Dev came off as such a carefree charmer that most people never noticed how truly guarded he was.

"You think I should forget it and move on," Lola Ann surmised.

"Hey, I'm the *last* person to judge when it comes to il-logical crushes," Ronnie insisted. Lola Ann knew her secret. With most guys in town, Ronnie could shoot the breeze about anything from spark plugs to the finer bluffing strategies of Texas Hold 'Em to the Titans' most recent football season. But there was one man who left her tongue-tied and uncomfortably aware that no one had taught her the feminine arts.

Jason McDeere. The high school English teacher who'd moved to Joyous last spring with his toddler daughter was unlike any of the other men Ronnie knew. While it was true they hadn't said more than a few words to each other, she couldn't help but feel a bond with him, given the losses he'd experienced.

"Hi, girls!" The throaty alto voice was instantly recognizable, and Ronnie was grinning even before she turned her head.

"Treble! Always good to see you, *Mrs. Caldwell.*" Ronnie emphasized the title with a wink.

"Absolutely," Lola Ann chimed in, "but I'm shocked to see you out and about. I figured newlyweds had better ways of spending their Friday nights than hanging with the likes of us."

Treble, a gorgeous brunette who towered over them, compliments of her spike heels, laughed good-naturedly. "Are you kidding? I go out of my way to find you two. At least neither of you resent me for taking Keith off the market." She punctuated this with a fond glance at her husband, who was ordering them drinks at the bar.

Though Treble had grown up in Joyous, she'd moved away years ago. When she'd returned to Tennessee over the summer, she'd won the heart of Dr. Keith Caldwell, one of the most sought-after men in town. To celebrate Valentine's Day, they'd eloped last month. Treble's family grumbled about her nontraditional ways, but Ronnie knew they were thrilled for her newfound happiness, especially Treble's sister, Charity. "Resent you?" Lola Ann echoed. "Heck, no. We want to live vicariously through you! Ronnie here hasn't had a date in—"

"Hey!" Ronnie interrupted her friend's impish tone. "Pot, kettle, very black."

Lola Ann grinned. "I meant to say, neither of us have had a date in ages. We're living out a different story from the whirlwind courtship, followed by impulsive elopement."

"So what's your story like?" Treble asked.

"The 'love from afar' kind," Lola Ann said, glancing furtively at Devin and the blonde.

Treble made a sympathetic face. "Have you tried telling him your feelings?"

"Of course not!" Lola Ann looked horrified. "That would defeat the 'afar' concept. Now, if you'll excuse me, I'm going to the ladies' room to freshen my lipstick before Treble talks me into something ludicrously bold that I'd regret tomorrow."

"What?" Treble widened her eyes in feigned innocence. "It's like you don't know me at all."

Ronnie snorted.

"So, what about you?" Treble asked, zeroing in on a fresh victim. "Have you considered telling Jason McDeere about your mad, secret love?"

Hell, no. "You exaggerate. I don't think you can call it love I barely know the man." Their very first conversation had been after Ronnie rammed into Jason with her shopping cart at the local grocery. She'd apologized, feeling clumsy and starstruck by his good looks. *Those eyes...* Someone with Treble's fearless poise had probably never had to maim a man to get his attention.

"Why not go talk to him now?" Treble prodded. "*Get* to know him."

"Now? You mean he's *here?*" Heat bloomed in Ronnie's face; she'd never been able to outgrow the blushing her brothers had teased her mercilessly about.

"In the flesh." Treble gestured toward the bar area and a row of tall narrow tables. "I passed him when I came over to say hello."

Ronnie had to look twice to make sure, but, yes, there was Jason McDeere, standing at one of the tables. What was he doing here? She'd been doing her best to keep the blues at bay, but if Jason were here on a date… There were two drinks on the table in front of Jason, but to her somewhat embarrassed relief, he seemed to be here with Coach Hanover, a forty-something man she knew mostly through his restoration of a classic '55 Ford F-100.

"This is your chance!" Treble nudged her. "In case I haven't said so before, you have excellent taste. He's gorgeous."

Ronnie nodded. "None of the teachers looked like that when *I* was a sophomore." Jason was somewhere between her height and that of her looming brothers. The lean, corded muscle was well defined in his arms, and the slim gold glasses he sometimes wore made his chiseled face even more masculine in contrast. He didn't have them on tonight, she noticed.

"So?" Treble prompted.

Ronnie's throat was so dry she could barely get her tongue unstuck from the roof of her mouth. "I wouldn't know what to say." With his quiet, reflective manner and literary profession, he was intriguingly different from her brothers and the other men she'd known all her life. *My brothers!* "Besides, Danny and Devin are both here. If they see me talking to Jason, they'll be on him like white on rice, wanting to know his net worth and his intentions."

Treble tilted her head, sending a cascade of dark spirals over one slim shoulder. "I know how protective they can be of you, but Danny seems nicely occupied with his wife and I don't even see Devin anymore. It's a thick crowd— seems like a good chance for a friendly hello without sibling interference. You want to know what I think?"

Ronnie grinned, despite the butterflies churning in her stomach like oversize mutant insects from an old grade-B horror movie. "Probably not."

"I think that, given your home situation when you were younger—" the gentle empathy in Treble's voice made it clear she was talking not just about the obnoxious brothers but about Ronnie's mom being sick "—you missed out on some of the formative opportunities to flirt and date that most girls, myself included, took for granted. And now you feel so daunted at the prospect that you cling to Dev and Danny as an excuse not to learn."

"That's—" Ronnie broke off, closed her mouth, opened it again, then finally admitted defeat with a quick shake of her head. "That's annoyingly insightful."

"Well, back in Atlanta, I did have my own radio advice show, remember?" These days, Treble co-anchored a regional cable morning show. It would never make her famous, but she seemed happy with her life.

Ronnie blew out a puff of air. When was the last time she'd felt truly happy? She was *content,* but that wasn't the same. Having lived her whole life in Joyous, she loved the town and the people in it—her friends, her family—but lately she'd had the growing, restless awareness of wanting more. Wanting… Almost involuntarily, her gaze strayed back to Jason McDeere. He looked up, and for just a heartbeat, their eyes met.

A potent zing went through her body. Then someone moved between them, and the moment was gone. Still, her reaction had been powerful enough to brook no doubt: she wanted Jason McDeere.

Ronnie squared her shoulders. "All right," she told Treble. "Pretend I'm someone who called in to your show for advice. Do you have any magical secrets for making me more…" What kind of woman did a man like Jason even want?

Experimentally, Ronnie tried to imagine what his wife had been like, but no one in town knew anything about her—only that newly divorced Jason had moved here to live with his grandmother and pick up the pieces of his life for himself and his daughter. Unfortunately, Sophie McDeere, a woman liked by all who'd known her, had passed away this winter. A wave of sympathy washed over Ronnie, nearly as forceful as the attraction she'd felt.

"You want me to start with the bare basics?" Treble asked.

"Use small words. And, if you want me to be able to concentrate, you should probably stand in my line of vision." She couldn't help stealing another peek at Jason. Despite Treble's can-do attitude, Ronnie suspected that any romantic involvement between her and Jason McDeere was nothing more than a pipe dream.

Yet, acknowledging that fact did remarkably little to slow her racing pulse.

"AHA!" COACH HANK HANOVER snapped his beefy fingers; he was the track coach for Joyous High, but his build was reminiscent of football. "I know the perfect woman."

"But—"

"Becca Gibbons, two o'clock. She's looked over at you a couple of times now."

Jason McDeere wasn't surprised the coach steamrolled over his objection. After all, Hank had once invited Jason and Emily for a barbecue that had turned out to be a blind-date ambush. Jason had overheard Caren Hanover just last month, insisting to her husband that they had to "find a good woman for that sweet man and his poor little girl." With Gran gone, it was as if the townspeople of Joyous had adopted him and were determined to improve his life...whether he wanted their help or not.

"Becca's the blonde in that group over there," Coach was saying. "Real nice gal, damn shame about her husband taking up with that woman from Nashville. Becca's a single mom, so y'all have plenty in common. Come on, you couldn't ask for a prettier dance partner!"

"I thought we came to play darts," Jason said. At least, that was the thin pretext used to get him here, though they hadn't been closer than fifty feet to the dartboard since they arrived.

Earlier, there'd been a pizza dinner at the Hanover house for the boys' and girls' track teams. Jason was an unofficial chaperone who knew most of the kids because he sometimes ran with the teams for exercise. The teenage girls had fussed over how cute Emily was, and, as the party wound down, his daughter had fallen asleep in the study during a *Shrek* showing. Caren had thrown her husband meaningful glances and Jason had allowed himself to be talked into a quick drink and round of darts.

"She'll be fine here for an hour," Caren had said, tucking a quilt around his daughter's shoulders. "Go out with Hank, take some 'you' time."

It was true that he hadn't indulged in much of a social life since Sophie's passing: Yet now that he stood in noisy Guthrie Dance Hall, where it seemed everyone but him had known one another since kindergarten, he couldn't believe he'd let himself get conned into another attempt to introduce him to eligible women.

"I'm sure Becca's lovely," Jason said, "but we've finished our drinks and should probably head back to your place."

The coach looked crestfallen. "You haven't danced with *anybody* yet."

"Hank, I appreciate the thought, but there's already a female in my life whom I love with my whole heart." In the past year and a half, Emily had been abandoned by her mother and moved to a new town, where she'd lost yet another maternal figure when Gran died in her sleep. His daughter needed time for her life to stabilize—his starting to date probably wasn't the best way to achieve that.

"A female?" Hank was a good man, but subtlety was lost on him. He squinted at Jason in confusion. "You don't mean your ex? 'Cause I thought that was done."

"It is. Completely." Jason had worked his way through the initial denial and shock of Isobel's departure to subsequent fury and eventual, faintly pitying, acceptance. He had no desire to pick at that particular emotional scab. "But just because I'm over *her* doesn't mean I'm eager to start the search for the future Mrs. McDeere."

"Okay, okay." The other man held up his hands in a gesture of surrender. "Had to try, though. I promised the wife. No hard feelings?"

"No, of c—" Jason stared past the coach's shoulder, meeting a pair of wide jade eyes. Logically, he knew he couldn't make out the woman's eye color from several yards away, but he'd seen her around town plenty of times. His memory automatically filled in the visual details that were fuzzy from this distance, as well as her name: Veronica Carter. Perhaps she'd merely been looking around, just as he had, and their gazes colliding was coincidence. But there seemed to be something in her expression—

A laughing couple wandered into his line of sight, blocking Veronica, and he blinked, feeling foolish.

"McDeere?"

"Yeah. Sorry, I just remembered something I needed to take care of Monday."

"Really? 'Cause it was more like you were staring at someone." Hank glanced over his shoulder, trying to confirm his suspicion.

"So, are we ready to leave?" Jason asked.

"I guess." But Hank wasn't completely diverted. "You *sure* you weren't looking at someone?"

Jason had never been good at lying outright. "Like who?"

His friend shrugged. "Dunno…but if there is someone who's caught your interest, I'll hear about it soon enough. One thing you'll learn about Joyous if you haven't already, it's damn near impossible to keep a secret here."

Chapter Two

"Mornin', darlin'."

Ronnie glanced up from the Monday paper she was scanning at the table and smiled as Wayne Carter came down the stairs into the kitchen. "Hey, Daddy."

"What's on the breakfast menu this morning?"

"Cereal." She pointed to the bowl and spoon she'd pulled out for him. "It's the one thing I'm guaranteed not to burn."

He paused behind her, ruffling her hair. "You're too hard on yourself. You've blossomed into a fair cook."

Well, she hadn't sent anyone to Doc Caldwell with food poisoning, so she guessed that was something.

She could hold her own with prepackaged meals and brownies made from a mix, but she couldn't duplicate the efforts of Sue Carter, who used to can her own jellies, made noodles from scratch for her soup and never once served a store-bought dessert until after her cancer diagnosis. One day, a few weeks after her mother's funeral, Ronnie had stood inside the walk-in pantry sobbing at the realization that they were about to open the last of mama's blackberry preserves and that there would never be any more.

The sounds of her dad's chair scraping on the tile and

subsequent rustling of cereal into a ceramic bowl dragged Ronnie back to the present. She blinked against the phantom sting of long-ago tears.

Wayne nodded toward the paper. "You done with the sports page?"

"You can have the whole thing."

The *Journal-Report* was folded in half, open to the classified section. Her dad glanced down, then back at her.

"I was, ah, looking for good deals on furniture I could restore."

"For the new place." To give him credit, he tried to sound happy for her. But there was no mistaking the shadow that passed over his expression. "It'll sure be lonely with you gone."

She rose, carrying her empty bowl to the sink. "You'll still have Dev."

Before Ronnie was born, Wayne and Sue had bought the converted farmhouse in which she'd lived her entire life. Though the surrounding acreage that comprised the original farm had been sold off in parcels to local families, the old bunkhouse sat at the back of Wayne's property. Devin had fixed it up and moved in, paying a nominal rent each month. Half the time, he joined them for dinner.

Or breakfast, if he hadn't entertained an overnight guest. *At least he has the freedom to* have *overnight guests.* Ronnie glared through the blue-checkered curtains in the direction of her brother's unseen home.

She rinsed the dishes, wiped her damp palms on the front of her jeans and smiled at her father. "Besides, you'll see me practically every day, boss."

He laughed. "True. You probably think I'm being an old fool, don't you? It's just…you're the last little bird to leave the nest."

Not that Devin had flown far, but she knew what her dad meant. Her brother Will had settled in North Carolina, where he'd gone to college and met his wife. Danny had Kaitlyn and Ashley now. Besides, restless Dev with his odd jobs and fleeting girlfriends sometimes seemed as likely to take off for a distant ranching job in Texas as show up for Sunday dinner. Her brothers, in their individual ways, were all living their lives.

Then there's me, caught in a time warp.

She worked for her father, lived at home and was so tongue-tied at the thought of asking a cute guy to dance that she might as well still be the awkward, freckled fifteen-year-old who wore her brothers' hand-me-down T-shirts more often than dresses. Even now, Lola Ann kidded that Ronnie only knew two hairstyles—a ponytail beneath her denim Carter & Sons cap and a ponytail without the hat. Glancing down, she took in the faded George Strait concert shirt she'd tucked into her jeans.

"I think I'll run and change before heading to the garage," she said, hearing the rueful note in her own voice.

Her dad paused with a spoonful of shredded wheat halfway to his mouth. "What the heck's wrong with what you're wearing?"

For the mechanic who'd be sliding on protective coveralls, anyway? Nothing. For the woman she'd started wondering if she would ever truly become? More than she could possibly articulate.

BY THE TIME JASON APPROACHED the front of the high school, his paper bag from the Sandwich Shoppe in hand, there wasn't much of his free period left to eat lunch at his desk. It would have been quicker to take his car, but the mid-March weather was ideal, providing the perfect sun-dappled, breezy backdrop for the picturesque town.

"Afternoon, Mr. McDeere." Allen, the custodian, stood a few feet away at the half wall that formed a horseshoe around the school's courtyard. Just beyond the brick wall were several picnic tables, the flagpole and the stairs leading inside.

Though the overall crime rate in Joyous was low, there had been some recent drive-by mailbox bashings and a spate of graffiti on the courtyard wall. Jason shook his head at the spray-painted suggestion that had appeared over the weekend. Obscene *and* misspelled.

"I see our miscreants are keeping you busy," Jason said.

Allen grinned beneath his bushy gray mustache. "Beats spending the day inside solving plumbing emergencies. Principal Schonrock's on the warpath, though. In the faculty lounge, she was threatening to cancel Spring Fling if the vandalism continues, but talked herself out of it, not wanting to penalize the whole student body for the actions of a few."

Spring Fling was the formal dance at the end of this month. Since Jason hadn't attended Homecoming in October or the Holiday Ball in December, Betty Schonrock had made it clear she expected Jason to take his turn and help chaperone the Fling. He'd gone so far as to promise his second-period class that if every one of them memorized either the Queen Mab speech from *Romeo and Juliet* or Mark Antony's address in *Julius Caesar,* Jason would hit the dance floor to bust some old school moves. All part of his ongoing attempts to get the students engaged in Shakespeare.

Plan B was to point out some of the more creative insults and dirty jokes in the Bard's plays, but Principal Schonrock might frown on that.

He took the stairs two at a time and had no sooner entered the building than he spotted the principal herself. She'd left the administrative office and was headed in the direction of the cafeteria. Betty was a diminutive but solidly built woman with a bob of silver-white hair and a sharp turquoise gaze that struck fear in the hearts of students, from pimply freshmen to linebackers on the Jaguar football team.

"Speak of the devil," Jason said as he fell in step with her.

She arched an eyebrow. "That had better be a figure of speech and not a character assessment."

"Yes, ma'am. Allen and I were just discussing the graffiti and your determination to end it."

"God as my witness, even if I have to camp out in the courtyard every night with a sleeping bag, thermos of coffee and an industrial-size flashlight, I'm going to catch someone in the act and make an example of them."

"Those kids don't know who they're messing with," he said affectionately. "I heard you even considered taking away Spring Fling."

Pausing, she slanted him a reproachful scowl. "Don't sound so hopeful, McDeere."

"Not at all. I'm…looking forward to it."

"Good." She nodded crisply before zeroing in on two girls standing near a bank of lockers. "Seneca, Jess. Do you ladies have some reason for loitering in the hallways?"

"We were on our way to the media center to work on a research project for Miss Burrows." The taller of the two answered while her friend spared a quick glance at Jason, then lowered her head, giggling. "We have a pass."

"Well, pick it up a little. I've seen injured turtles move faster than that."

The girls both nodded, skirting around the principal to make their way down the corridor. Whispers and laughter trailed after them. Though he hoped it was his imagination, Jason thought he caught his name.

Principal Schonrock assessed him, arms akimbo. "About that spring formal, McDeere, I don't suppose you'll be bringing a date?"

"Ma'am?" He was unprepared for the random question, though he assumed *she* wasn't asking him out. Mr. Schonrock wouldn't approve.

"A date, McDeere. A female companion to whom you bring cups of ginger ale punch between rounds on the dance floor."

What was it with the people in this town and their preoccupation with his social life? "I plan to go stag. Stay focused on the kids, make sure no one smuggles a flask to spike the punch."

"I've got punch duty, no worries there." She sighed. "You're one of the best literature teachers we've ever had at this school, but you do pose the occasional problem."

"Such as?" Jason was genuinely baffled, but open to constructive criticism if it would improve his effectiveness in the classroom.

For perhaps the first time since he'd known her, Betty seemed hesitant, glancing down the hall, checking in both directions before she replied. "When you were helping Coach Hanover with the cross-country team last semester, did you happen to notice how many divorced moms showed up at meets?"

"They were there to support their kids."

"Some of them didn't have kids on the team. Some of them didn't even have kids at this school! Then there's my own faculty. Shannon Cross has been teaching for four years and never once wore a low-cut sweater to a PTA meeting before you joined the staff. The way she and Leigh Norris bat their eyelashes at you over the coffeepot makes them seem more like students than educators. And it's affected their professional relationship. Last Friday, I thought there might actually be a catfight."

"Er…" While he wasn't comfortable with the increasingly flirtatious mannerisms of his two female colleagues, he was even less comfortable discussing them with the principal. "Maybe it would be better to have this chat with Ms. Cross and Ms. Norris."

"I have. But it's not just them. You stand out conspicuously. We have a small staff here and very few male teachers. Aside from you, *no* male teachers who are single."

"That has no bearing on my job performance."

"Of course not, but you saw how Seneca and Jess reacted to you."

"Teenage girls giggle all the time," he said stiffly.

"Last week, Mrs. Feeney walked into the D Hall restroom and overheard three girls making dares on ways to get your attention. I dealt with it, but the fact of the matter remains that some parents…"

Surely no one had ever accused him of flirting with

student? If he didn't resent the implication so much, he might have laughed at the irony. He hadn't wanted to be single! When he'd made the vow to stay with Isobel until death parted them, he'd meant it. He just hadn't anticipated her bailing on motherhood and, consequently, their marriage.

He tightened his grip on his lunch, probably crushing the sandwich inside the sack. "Principal Schonrock, I don't like the tone of this conversation. If you'll excuse me, I only have a few minutes left before the bell rings."

"Jason, I'm sorry I've upset you. I considered not telling you about the restroom incident at all, but thought it better if you knew."

"So that I can bring a date to the Spring Fling?" There were limits on what he was willing to do in his personal life to appease those in charge of his professional life.

"It might not hurt if people thought of you as less available."

He bared his teeth in a humorless smile, spelling out what he'd tried to make Coach Hanover understand the other night. "I am the sole caretaker of a two-year-old. With my grandmother gone, I've tailored my schedule around Emily's sitter and have been struggling in my nonexistent spare time, between potty training and grading papers, to renovate the run-down house Gran left us. Trust me, I'm about as *un*available as you can get."

"MMM." LOLA ANN CLOSED HER eyes briefly, tilting her face up toward the sun, clearly a woman who'd never freckled. "Days as lovely as today, I wonder why anyone ever drives."

"Hey!" Ronnie laughed, scooting over on the sidewalk

to avoid the dropped remains of an ice cream cone. "That's my job security you're threatening. How would you like it if I started questioning why people still read books?"

"Not enough of them do," Lola Ann said vehemently.

"You have a point." Certainly the men in Ronnie's family never read anything unless it was related to sports or automobiles. She made a mental note to include a children's book along with whatever gift she gave her niece for her next birthday.

A memory surfaced, the Christmas her freshman year when her dad and brothers had bought her a stack of cookbooks. *The only kitchen tools I'll need after the move are a microwave, a can opener and a refrigerator magnet with the phone number of the town's pizza-delivery place.*

It wasn't that she'd ended up stuck with traditionally female chores because her brothers were meat-headed chauvinists. Juggling schoolwork and, in the case of Danny and Will, part-time jobs, they'd all helped around the house in different ways while Wayne ran the garage. Struggling to fulfill a promise that first year after Mom's death, Ronnie had inadvertently set the pattern from which she still hadn't broken free.

Take care of them. Looking back, Ronnie knew what her mother had meant—after all, without feminine interference, Will and Devin might never have thought to put on clean clothes. Yet, Ronnie felt as if she'd spent more time trying ineptly to fill someone else's shoes than finding her own footsteps.

The library was on the corner, and Ronnie automatically slowed, assuming this was where she and Lola Ann would part company after their lunch.

"I, um, thought I'd walk with you," Lola Ann said. "You know, work off some of that barbecue. Plus, I have to go to the post office. The garage is on the way."

Ronnie raised her eyebrows but didn't comment on her friend's indirect route. "Suit yourself, I'm happy for the company."

While Joyous was by and large a rural community where cars were a necessity, the few blocks of "downtown," with its old-fashioned storefronts and limited parking, really did make for a nice stroll. They ran into numerous acquaintances, including Charity Sumner as she exited Claudette's Beauty Salon.

"Charity!" Navigating the stroller the blonde pushed, Ronnie gave her a one-armed hug. "Long time, no see."

Charity was Treble's younger sister and, next to Lola Ann, Ronnie's closest friend.

"We've missed you at Guthrie's, but understand what's kept you so busy." Lola Ann leaned down to admire eight-month-old Brooke. "A cutie like this one sure makes the biological clock tick louder."

Ronnie shifted her weight, listening as the other two women discussed baby milestones. Truthfully, Ronnie's biological clock wasn't running all that fast. She doubted it was even plugged in.

"I should be going." Charity glanced at her watch reluctantly. "But we have to get together soon! Now that she's sleeping through the night and I don't constantly feel like a zombie, it's time to reclaim my life."

After they'd said goodbye, her friend's words kept looping in Ronnie's mind, like one of those irritatingly catchy pop songs that are impossible to get out of your

head. *Time to reclaim my life, time to reclaim my life.* It wa
exactly how Ronnie had been feeling...except, had she
ever created a life to reclaim?

"Lola Ann, is twenty-five too old for deciding what you
want to be when you grow up?"

"What? I thought you liked being a mechanic."

"I do. I meant metaphorically rather than professionally."

Frankly, she'd never analyzed her vocational choice too
closely. Wayne, who'd inherited the garage from his own
father, had spoken often of sharing the place with his boys.
Danny was the bookkeeper and worked in a mostly administrative capacity, although he'd probably help with basic
maintenance procedures this week because people were
gearing up for spring break road trips, keeping them busier
than usual. Devin was a certified mechanic, but only pitched
in between construction jobs to supplement his income—
Joyous wasn't a hotbed of new buildings and roadways. Of
Wayne's four children, Ronnie was the only one to become
a full-time mechanic at the annoyingly named Carter & Sons.

She glared up at the sign that had never really bothered
her before now.

Then she shook her head, trying to clear away the nega-
tivity. "Honest to God, I don't know what's wrong with me
lately. I've been cranky. Itchy in my own skin, bad
tempered and unable to sleep."

"Maybe it's sexual frustration," her friend teased.
"That's made *me* peevish on more than one occasion."

"The sad part is, you're probably right." Ronnie
glanced back up at the familiar sign and sucked in a deep
breath. "Lola Ann, it's time to make some changes. Are
you with me?"

The brunette looked nervous. "Uh…with you on what, exactly?"

"We've got to take charge of our lives." Running into Charity today had reinforced the realization that most of the people Ronnie knew were moving forward in different ways. Buying her house was an important step, but it didn't have to be the only one. "You're a bright, attractive woman. You don't have to get all your happily ever afters from books—create your own future. If you're really interested in that brother of mine, make him notice you. The next time I see Jason at Guthrie Hall, I am marching up to him and claiming that dance I've always wanted."

"You are?" Lola An asked skeptically.

"I am! And if I can be brave, so can you."

"Seems awfully convenient that the theoretical object of your bravery almost never comes to Guthrie's."

"I'm aiming for greatness here, don't distract me with minor problems like reality."

Lola Ann laughed. "All right. After you, o fearless leader."

Empowered, Ronnie swung open the door. Lola Ann followed her inside the small office area that opened via a carpeted hallway into the much larger repair bays. "I'm back from lunch!"

Danny glanced up from his computer, looking amused at her inexplicably emphatic tone. "So we see."

"'Bout time you got back, slacker." Devin passed them en route from the minifridge, a carton of leftover take-out food in his hand. "Hey, Lola Ann." He punctuated his greeting by affectionately chucking her chin, a gesture of such asexual fondness that Ronnie almost winced on her friend's behalf.

Lola Ann's expression was one of abject misery. Devin being male and clueless, missed it completely.

"Well, I'll let you get back to work," Lola Ann told her friend. "I've gotta get to the post office, pick up those stamps."

"We'll see you on Saturday for dinner." Ronnie gave her an encouraging smile. "In the meantime, don't forget what we discussed. The world really can be your oyster."

Turning to go, Lola Ann raised a halfhearted fist in solidarity.

"We make our own destiny," Ronnie called through the door as it closed. "Even the most daunting journeys start with one decisive step!"

Devin stared at her. "Someone had way too many fortune cookies at lunch. What was that about?"

"Nothing you need worry your pretty head over," Ronnie said. "Is Dad in the back?"

"Went to lunch with one of his poker buddies," Danny answered, his eyes never leaving the monitor.

So it was just her and her brothers? She bit her lip, recalled this morning and decided to take advantage of the opportunity. "Devin, after I move out, will you go by the house for dinners and stuff? Keep him company."

"I suppose, as long as it doesn't put a crimp in my social life." When he saw that she was seriously concerned, he sobered. "Sure, no prob. You know I always pop in to do my laundry, anyway." The bunkhouse didn't have a washer and dryer.

Ronnie rolled her eyes. "I assume you refer to the bags of clothes you leave on the laundry room floor that get magically sorted, washed and folded for you."

"Yeah, gotta love those laundry fairies." Grinning, he speared a bite of cold pasta.

"Well, this laundry fairy is about to get her own mortgage payments," she snapped, "so you're going to have to learn how to measure out detergent."

Devin blinked. "Hey…I didn't think you minded. I mean, you were doing yours and dad's clothes so I figured it was no trouble to toss in one other person's. I wasn't trying to take advantage of you, Red."

"Don't worry about it." She waved a hand, feeling shrewish. "Just, now that I'm moving out, things will have to change." Actually, *her* house didn't come with a washer and dryer, so maybe she could go to Dad's house once a week and— No! She would save her quarters and use a Laundromat, or take pizza and a DVD to Lola Ann's and do a couple of loads there.

They'd snagged Danny's attention; he was peering at her intently. "You okay, sis? You seem wound pretty tight."

No way was she sharing Lola Ann's theory about why that might be.

"I'm excited about the move, but a little stressed, too," Ronnie said. "It might be weird, not living in my room anymore."

"It'll be an adjustment," he agreed. "For Dad, too. Maybe we could get him a puppy for Easter or something."

"Do you think…" She swallowed, thinking of their father's increasingly forlorn moods. "Has he ever considered dating?"

Neither of her brothers replied, but they both looked pointedly at the single framed snapshot on Wayne's desk.

Danny glanced back at Ronnie, his expression both

poignant and proud. "You look so much like her." As the oldest, he'd had the most years with Sue, the most stored memories.

Ronnie laughed self-consciously. "Oh, right. I can see her now, standing in the kitchen in shapeless coveralls with a grease smudge on her cheek."

"Flour." Devin interjected. "I'd come home from school to the smell of something amazing baking, and she'd have little smears of flour on her skin and apron. God, she made the house smell good."

Better than I ever did, Ronnie thought with an apologetic pang.

Silence fell over the little room, and Ronnie didn't know who was more discomfited by the thick undercurrent of sentiment—the guys, or her.

Danny cleared his throat. "Guess who brought her car in while you were at lunch? Beth Gold. Seems her vehicle is suffering from phantom engine noises again."

Ronnie was grateful for the excuse to laugh. "You mean those noises no one else has ever heard but which always seem to mysteriously reappear if she notices Dev working the shop?"

"I don't think it's engine noises," Danny said solemnly. "I think it's lo-o-o-ve."

At this, Devin harrumphed. "We went on two dates this summer. Two! She should let it go."

"She can't," Danny said. "Because she's in lo-o-o-ve."

Devin tossed a wadded-up napkin at his older brother, doing his part to dispel the earlier emotional tension. "Does Kaitlyn know that when you're away from her good influence, you revert to a ten-year-old?"

"At least I've learned how to be a grown-up part of the time. Just one of the benefits of life with a good woman," Danny said. "Something you would discover if you settled down."

"There's the problem," Devin said. "Why 'settle' when I can get to know so many different beautiful women, each with her own delightful and unique personality?"

"Yeah, 'cause it's really their *personalities* you're after, you hound."

Devin jerked his head meaningfully toward Ronnie, apparently wanting to spare her delicate sensibilities. Then he smiled, taking the opportunity to redirect Danny's brotherly concern. "If you want someone in the family to find domestic bliss, you should stop badgering me and help Ronnie here."

Ronnie ground her teeth and grabbed some paperwork from the inbox on Danny's desk. "I don't need 'help.'"

"Sure you do," Devin said. "How long's it been since you had a date?"

"My darling siblings run off my potential dates."

"That's not true!" Devin protested. "We just screen them carefully. To keep away those who aren't good enough."

Danny nodded. "The guys who wouldn't be right for you in the long run, the guys who are too stupid to know how to change their own oil, the guys who only have One Thing in mind."

"You mean like Dev?" she asked wryly.

"Exactly!" Devin flashed an unrepentant smile, then grimaced. "God forbid you go out with anyone like me. If you did, we'd have to kill him. You don't want Kaitlyn and Ashley reduced to visiting Danny in prison, do you?"

It was time Ronnie got to work on a car. Interlocking automotive systems made far more sense than her knucklehead brothers. Besides, she felt like taking something apart with her hands. But Danny calling her name in a soft voice stopped her in the doorway.

She looked over her shoulder with mild curiosity. "Yes?"

"There isn't someone...specific you'd like to date, is there?" he asked. "Someone like, well, Jason McDeere."

"Jason McWho?" She felt herself go white. Literally felt all the blood drain from her face in an almost audible whoosh.

Danny held her gaze. "After we had dinner at Adam's Ribs last week, Kaitlyn mentioned that you were watching Jason."

Darn her sister-in-law's keen powers of observation! "I was just admiring what a good father he is to that little girl," Ronnie mumbled.

"See?" Devin's posture relaxed. "She was melting over the kid, not the guy. Her biological clock's probably in countdown mode."

She was going to clock the next person who used that phrase! Still, hard to argue without invalidating her own alibi.

"But Kaitlyn said you were looking at McDeere the way I used to look at my old Thunderbird."

Devin shook his head. "As much as I adore your wife, Danny-boy, I think she's off base. McDeere's a decent sort, but a high school English teacher? Not the most manly job, reading Lord Bryan and Edgar Allen Poe to kids all day."

"It's Lord *Byron*," Ronnie snapped. "And how is shaping the minds of today's youth and, by extension, the future of our country, somehow inferior to selling wiper fluid? Just because he doesn't spend his time belching or

scratching or chasing skirts at Guthrie Hall like you…
Jason McDeere is an intelligent, charming, good-looking
man, and any woman in town would be lucky to have him.

"Really good-looking," she added in a breathless after-
thought, temporarily recalling those eyes and that smile
instead of her audience: two brothers who were now gaping.

"Well, I'll be," Devin said. "Kaitlyn was right."

A slow smile spread across Danny's face. "Ronnie's in
-o-o-o-ve."

"We may have to screen him," Devin said thoughtfully.

"You stay away from Jason McDeere or I will bludgeon
you unconscious with a crescent wrench!" On the heels of that
threat, Ronnie spun around and headed for the repair bays.

Her interfering, overprotective brothers knew about her
attraction to Jason. What were the odds that they wouldn't
mention it to her equally overprotective father? Ronnie
groaned, inhaling the scent of gasoline and industrial
cleaners. Was it too late to fake her own death, skip out of
town and start a new life far from Joyous?

Preferably, a life *without* siblings.

Chapter Three

"Wiseshine, Daddy!"

Even from his nearly unconscious state, Jason was able to translate Emily's message of *rise and shine*—a phrase he'd made the mistake of using sometime in the past. Because she liked the sound of it, his nearly three-year-old daughter used it frequently, whether it was technically appropriate or not. It would be more appropriate now, for instance, if the sun were actually up.

He cracked one eye open. "Morning, sweet pea." The digital clock on the nightstand said that it was 6:26 a.m. His little girl hadn't grasped the concept of sleeping in on the weekends and loved to bounce out of her toddler bed first thing Saturday.

At times like this, he really missed the retired crib where she'd been confined to playing with her stuffed animals until at least seven. Was it wrong to keep your kid behind bars so you could get an extra half hour of sleep?

Emily was struggling to hoist herself onto the double bed that dominated what had once been Sophie McDeere' guest room. The lavender wallpaper with its climbing vines of faded flowers had hung in here since his father was a boy.

Jason scooped his daughter up next to him and reached for the remote control nestled between the phone and the clock. While he hadn't bothered to bring the queen bed he'd once shared with his ex-wife to Joyous, he'd brought all the electronics, like the first-class stereo system, the DVD player and the large television that sat on the rose faux-marble top of a white wooden dresser.

Stifling a yawn, he smiled at his daughter. "How about I find some cartoons?" Maybe she wouldn't mind if he watched them from behind closed eyelids.

"'Kay." She snuggled closer, instantly agreeable as long as she got to be in his company.

As it so often did, the fact that he was all she had weighed heavily on his shoulders. Sometimes he worried that Emily was more clingy than other kids her age, but who could blame her? Her own mother, after months of an extreme postpartum depression, had shoved a crying baby into Jason's arms one day and walked out, never to return. More recently, "Gran-Gran" had, as Emily solemnly put it, gone to live in the sky. It was entirely possible Em would grow up with a few abandonment issues. Hell, after the way his marriage ended, *he* had abandonment issues.

He'd been fully aware of Isobel's depression and escalating panic that she wasn't cut out for motherhood, but he'd been trying his damnedest to help her through it, to solidify them as a family. He'd failed.

He refused to do so again. *We'll make it work, kiddo. I swear I'll do everything I can to be a good father.* He dropped a kiss on the top of her head, breathing in the grape smell of her no-tears children's shampoo. God, life should be like that. He should be able to protect this trusting little person curled into his side, be able to guarantee that everything would always come up smelling sweet, with limited tangles or tears.

For this morning, at least, she was coping better than him. While he spent twenty minutes worrying about all the ways he might potentially screw up as a parent, his daughter laughed—that unabashed, full-bodied sound that had taken him by surprise when she was a baby—at the antics of an animated rabbit and duck on the TV screen. Afterward, he made them a modest but healthy breakfast of cereal and strawberries.

"You get to see Zoë today," he reminded her as he buckled her into her booster seat at the table.

The Spencers across the street had a four-year-old daughter. Emily had always loved having the older girl over or even playing in the Spencers' yard when Jason stayed in view. It was only in the past couple of weeks that she'd consented to being in Mrs. Spencer's care without Jason there; even then, he kept his cell phone within reach in case Em suddenly and vehemently changed her mind, the way children her age could. While people often referenced the "terrible twos," he'd only seen real tantrums from Emily in the past month, and Wanda Spencer agreed that the worst trouble she ever had with Zoë was the transition from two to about four months after she turned three. Emily's third birthday would fall just after Easter this year.

Today, Wanda was taking the two girls to see a new G-rated movie at King Cinema that was garnering rave reviews from parents. The outing would give Jason a chance to run by the hardware store and pick up his latest batch of supplies. Though he knew more about elements of myth than he did wiring ceiling fans, modernizing this house meant something special to him. His dad had been in the military, and the family had relocated from base to base throughout Jason's childhood with Gran's place serving as a touchstone, a nostalgic constant. During the winter they'd lived in Alaska, Jason's mom had vowed that while she'd dutifully follow her husband all over the world during his career, once he retired, they were moving some-where very, very warm. They now resided in Phoenix. With her only child out west and her husband passing away several years ago, Sophie McDeere hadn't had much help keeping up with repairs on this place.

Until he'd returned to his lifelong refuge during the divorce proceedings, Jason hadn't realized how much the house had suffered from neglect. He'd made it his unspoken mission to respectfully refurbish Gran's place and, in the process, build a wonderful home for Emily. Of course, while he was learning as much as he could through various instruction manuals and painstaking trial, he didn't have a knack for design. If he let Emily have input, she'd probably insist on pink for everything from the sofa cushions to the carpet. There were some projects that needed…more of a woman's touch.

Sighing, he loaded their breakfast dishes into the washer, thinking about the magazine-perfect house he'd left behind. Isobel, always flawlessly put together, had had a natural talent for design. While pregnant, she'd decorated a baby nursery that looked like something out of a fairy tale. But no amount of unicorn switch plates or fanciful wall murals could make up for what Emily had lost.

Pushing aside thoughts of the past and his occasional demons of self-doubt, he helped his daughter get dressed and read her a few of her favorite picture books. Though he was unquestionably biased, he thought she had a great vocabulary for her age, which he attributed to the stories they shared. Afterward, they played in the yard until it was time to walk her over to the Spencers'.

He took Emily's hand as they climbed the four steps to the spacious front porch, where one of Zoë's dolls sat in the glider-swing. "Are you excited about the movie, sweet pea?"

She nodded and said something about princesses, which he understood was a major selling point to the female pre-school demographic. Emily was rarely without the tiara that had been part of the Halloween costume Gran put together for her. But despite his daughter's eagerness for the princess film, he noticed her glance nervously his way when Wanda Spencer opened the screen door. Would Em fuss when he left? During the week when he went to work, she stayed home with a mother of two who had her days free while her own sons were in school. Emily still cried about half the time when he left, and it continued to break his heart. He'd hoped she'd be better adjusted to her daytime caregiver, Miss Nina, by now.

Wanda Spencer had plenty of experience with little girls, however. She bent down to Emily's level, overlooking the girl's wide green eyes and trembling bottom lip. "Hey there. Zoë and I were just talking about how we couldn't wait for you to come over. She wants to show you a special bubble-blowing toy she got. We have plenty of time to play out back before our movie. Want to see?"

After a brief hesitation, Emily nodded, managing a smile when Zoë appeared in the doorway behind her mom.

As he watched the two little girls greet each other, Jason couldn't help making visual comparisons. Emily's dark hair was sliding out of the ponytail he'd attempted, and there was a sticky spot of strawberry residue he'd missed on her chin. Her clothes were clean, but her favorite green T-shirt, scuffed sneakers and purple skirt, worn over pull-up training pants, didn't quite have the panache of Zoë's pink-and-white shirt underneath pink overalls. She'd accessorized with pink-sparkle tennis shoes and ribbons at the end of two fancy braids. French braids? Braided pigtails? They reminded him of Dorothy's hair at the beginning of *The Wizard of Oz*. Did mothers take some sort of special class to learn how to do stuff like that? Plaiting 101. Every time he picked up the small lavender brush to fix Em's hair, he was all thumbs.

"She'll be fine," Wanda Spencer said, misreading his expression. "You go ahead, and we'll see you this afternoon."

"Thanks." He hugged Emily in farewell and turned to Zoë's mother. "Really, thank you."

The people in Joyous were nosy and interfering, no doubt about it, but they were also generous of spirit and especially quick to help those they considered part of the fold. He knew that in a town this size, you could go a long while and still be thought of as an outsider, but Sophie had been well loved and locals had automatically extended that affection to him. He should try harder to remember this feeling of warm gratitude the next time someone was telling him about a woman he just *had* to meet.

"You're welcome." Wanda touched his arm, briefly,

companionably. "I can't imagine how hard it must be to go it alone. Zoë's a good kid, but if I didn't have Brad to help me… Well, I hope you and Emily know we're here for whatever you need."

As he walked back across the street, he found himself hoping that Wanda didn't regret the open-ended offer of assistance. It was already becoming clear he'd have a lot of questions to deal with. Now that he was working with Emily on the concept of potty training and she was old enough to start voicing questions, he was increasingly aware of situations that he, as someone of the opposite gender, didn't feel equipped to handle.

Recalling Principal Schonrock's entreaties to bring a date to the Spring Fling, Jason made a face. He needed a woman, all right—not for some school dance, but someone who could braid hair and tackle delicate scenarios with a light touch. Emily was growing so fast that, before he knew it, she'd be a young woman getting her first—

Sheer panic filled him, so he squelched the thought immediately. Toddlerhood was terrifying enough; he didn't even want to contemplate puberty. *One day at a time.* It wasn't the most original or inspiring motto, but it had brought him this far. Whatever life threw at him next, he'd handle.

His daughter was counting on him.

SINCE SHE WASN'T SCHEDULED to work this particular Saturday, Ronnie had planned to use today to pack. Yet it had taken depressingly little time to box up her belongings.

Her father had shocked her that morning when he'd suggested she take the dining room table and china cabinet with her. "Your mama would've wanted to you to have them."

"Oh, I can't!" She'd glanced around the room, appalled by the thought of a big empty space. "I appreciate the thought, Daddy, but my place is too small. Besides, where would everyone sit at Thanksgiving and Easter and plain ol' family dinners?"

Speaking of this evening's looming supper... Her brothers had been suspiciously silent on the subject of Jason McDeere since teasing her at the beginning of the week. *Lulling you into a false sense of security, no doubt.* Heckling was a Carter family tradition, and she wondered what might be said later. Especially since in-sightful Kaitlyn, who had first clued Danny in about Ronnie's unspoken feelings, would be present. Ronnie still couldn't believe her sister-in-law had said anything without first broaching the subject with Ronnie herself. Sharing thoughts with a spouse must trump gal-pal confidences.

At any rate, there wasn't much left to pack that she wouldn't need between now and the move, so Ronnie decided to get out of the house for a few hours. Cranking up an old Bon Jovi CD she'd found while emptying out her desk, she drove to the town's main hardware supply store. She wanted to start thinking about the specific changes she planned to make, putting together a list of priorities and a preliminary budget.

Once inside the spacious warehouse, she grabbed a cart. Armed with a notepad of scribbled measurements and a calculator, she began at the far left, intending to make her way systematically across the aisles. She was only four rows in, however, when she halted. Her breath caught in her throat.

Jason McDeere.

He was standing in front of a section of white plastic strips dotted in colorful squares representing paint shades. Apparently he was interested in one of the color schemes on a lower shelf, because he'd bent over for a closer look. She couldn't help but notice the way the denim of his jeans—

"Veronica." He straightened, giving her a smile that was just a touch self-conscious.

"Hello." *Too formal.* "Hi." Yeah, that was better. "Hi." Except that now she'd greeted him three times and was probably coming off as manic. On the plus side, anything she said from here on out was bound to be an improvement as long as she didn't say it in triplicate. "How's it going?"

"Okay, I guess." He ran a hand through that thick hair— light brown with touches of burnished gold. "I consider myself an educated man, but hell if I can tell you the difference between 'apricot' and 'tangerine.' Or 'cranberry' and 'pomegranate.'"

She laughed, a combination of nerves and genuine amusement. "Are you wanting to paint something, or make a fruit salad?"

"Exactly!" Moving closer, he extended a strip with various shades of green. "Kiwi? Honeydew? They can't just call it yellow-green?"

"Maybe they thought they could charge more for honeydew."

He nodded, studying the selection in front of him with befuddled exasperation. "I always thought choice was a good thing, but this is overwhelming. Where do I start?

Now I know how my students feel when I tell them to pick a topic for their research paper each semester."

"You could try flipping a coin. It's what my brother Dev would do." But she was secretly pleased that Jason approached decisions more thoughtfully.

"Better yet, I could get a second opinion. Help a guy out, Veronica?"

Something rippled through her, a foreign intimacy at hearing her name again from his lips. "Actually, it's just Ronnie. Hardly anyone's called me Veronica since my mom died."

"Ronnie, then." After a moment, he asked gently, "Do you still miss her?"

"Some days more than others." Was he thinking of his grandmother? "Have I ever told you how sorry I was for your loss? Sophie was a lovely person."

He smiled. "She was, wasn't she? I like to think she's with Grandpa Bert now. I don't think she ever truly got over him."

Ronnie thought back to the photo of her mom in her dad's office. "Some people really do find that once-in-a-lifetime true love, don't they?"

This time, his smile was tinged with the barest hint of bitterness. "I might be the wrong person to ask."

Stupid, she chided herself. In light of his divorce, her babbling was probably insensitive. "So, um, paint samples?" Smooth segue. *Yeah, it's a real mystery why* you *never date.*

He glanced down at the stick in his hand as if he'd forgotten he held it. "Right. I've been putting off drastic changes to Gran's house because it seemed somehow disrespectful to her memory, but I can't ignore the needed repairs. There's one section of the roof I should reinforce so we don't end up with a leak, and the whole place could use some updating. My bedroom definitely needs a change."

Mine, too. It needs a man in it. Ronnie blinked, as horrified by the uncensored thought as if she'd said it aloud. She tried to squelch the idea, but when she glanced into Jason's eyes her nebulous fantasies took on new clarity. She couldn't remember the last time she'd cursed her redhead's fair complexion so thoroughly. He'd have to be blind not to notice she was blushing. There was a question in his eyes, but he didn't voice it.

Doing her best to sound nonchalant, she asked, "Then you're planning to paint your room?"

"Probably. The wallpaper that's in there now has got to go. No offense to Gran's taste, but I'm not really a roses kind of guy."

She smiled. "When I was seven, my mother painted my room pink, hung frilly white curtains and got lacy pillow covers for my bed."

"Sounds like my daughter's idea of heaven," he said.

"Yeah, well, *I* coveted the monster truck decor in Will's room. So I empathize on not loving the roses." It occurred to her that as lone occupant of her new house, she could fix up the entire place in a monster-truck motif. She chuckled at the image.

Jason raised an eyebrow. "What's funny?"

"It's silly."

"Try me. I have a two-year-old, I'm fluent in silly."

"I'm buying my first house this week," she said. Just saying it out loud sent joy glowing through her. "I suddenly pictured all the rooms done in that truck theme I wanted when I was a kid."

He grinned. "I'm starting to think maybe I *shouldn't* ask your decorating advice."

"Definitely not. I'm doing well just to pick out clothes each morning that don't actively clash."

"Looks like you do okay." As he spoke, his eyes swept downward in automatic observation. Yet long before he'd reached her navy shirt and white shorts, his gaze slowed, became something less casual and more reflective.

Her skin tingled in the wake of his visual caress. She was unused to prolonged perusal from a man, was even less accustomed to the elemental admiration she saw dawning in those indescribable eyes. Her heart sped up in her chest, and she wondered if he could make out the rapid flutters beneath the thin cotton.

She swallowed. "Thank you." It should have been a simple acknowledgment of a perfunctory compliment, but it was something more than that, husky and personal.

His eyes returned to hers, the expression in them dazed. A thrill of heady, feminine power shot through her—*she'd* put that look on Jason McDeere's face. It was surreal, so unexpected that she found herself emboldened enough to blurt, "Would you like to go have lunch with me?"

He hesitated, and she felt sure he would say no. After all, he'd just finished telling her how much work he had to do revamping his—

"I'd love to." His smile was boyish. "I'm as bad as my students. I always tell them not to procrastinate, but when faced with the prospect of slogging through more paint samples or a meal with a pretty girl… Well, it's a no-brainer. You've rescued me from a kiwi-pomegranate-tangerine meltdown."

In turn, *he'd* rescued *her* from going to bed tonight with the heavy feeling that she'd let one more day pass her by, full of quiet longings and missed opportunities.

Chapter Four

They crossed the parking lot toward Jason's car, a small four-door that got good mileage and consistently high consumer ratings, and he asked Ronnie if she had a specific restaurant in mind.

Hardly—she was making this up as she went along. "Have you tried out the new one a couple of streets over, near the drugstore?"

The establishment had changed management multiple times, trying to find its place in the culinary community. It had briefly been a barbecue joint (put out of business by the superior Adam's Ribs), a pizzeria, an Irish pub and—for about a week and a half—a sushi bar. Turned out, the citizens of this particular Tennessee town weren't clamoring for sashimi and unagi. Ronnie kind of missed the wasabi, though.

He opened the passenger door for her. "I haven't been there yet, but I'm game if you are."

"I have no idea what kind of menu to expect. How do you feel about surprises?"

His grin was wry. "Some are more welcome than others."

As soon as they walked into the restaurant, Jason indicated a framed oil painting of a dark-haired woman in a white cotton dress, which hung next to a sequined black velvet mariachi sombrero. "I'll go out on a limb and guess they serve Mexican."

A blonde with a bright smile met them, two laminated menus tucked against her chest. "Welcome to Tennessee Tacos, y'all." Her hair had been pulled back in a sleek topknot, a large silk flower pinned to the side, and she was dressed much like the woman in the painting.

Tennessee Tacos? Ronnie followed the hostess to an orange booth, sending a silent prayer heavenward that this wouldn't turn out to be a disaster.

There were actually quite a few patrons inside, although it was always difficult here to tell whether crowds were pulled in by great food or morbid curiosity. However, after her first bite of complimentary salsa—which cleared her sinuses and made her eyes water—Ronnie decided this place got her stamp of approval.

Yow. She grabbed the glass in front of her.

"Too hot for you?" Jason tried some, then reached for his own water.

"On the contrary, it's perfect. I like it hot."

If she were someone like Treble, she could imbue the words with flirty double entendre. But playing femme fatale just wasn't in her repertoire. Still, here she was, with Jason McDeere smiling at her across the table.

"A girl after my own heart," he said approvingly. "Em and I eat mostly bland fare—cut-up chicken, buttered noodles, applesauce. Now that she's past the baby-food stage, I've fallen out of the habit of cooking just for me."

She swiped another chip through the salsa. "I know

what you mean. The guys are picky eaters, and I gave up trying to broaden their vegetable horizons years ago." They humored her by eating green beans but drew the line at some of her favorites, like asparagus. Her monster-truck house was going to be a green-bean-free zone.

"The guys?" Jason parroted.

"My brothers. Of course Will and Danny moved out and are both married now, so I guess I mean Devin and my dad."

Ronnie had been so focused on the man seated across from her that the waitress seemed to materialize out of nowhere. "Sorry about the wait, you folks ready to order?"

"Uh…" Ronnie had completely forgotten to look at the menu, too engrossed in finally having a real conversation with Jason. She scanned the lunch specials, and an item caught her eye. "Steak fajitas for me."

Jason nodded. "Make that fajitas for two, please."

After they'd completed their order, Ronnie returned to their earlier topic. "What about you, any siblings?" It was funny how many tidbits she'd compiled about Jason, such as his habit of running his hand through his hair (gleaned from multiple observations) and how much he loved German chocolate cake (which Sophie had once told her while they waited for their numbers to be called at the bakery) without knowing the basic facts about him.

"Nope, only child."

"Lucky," she muttered.

He laughed. "It got lonely sometimes, especially since we moved so much. I've always wanted brothers or sisters for Em."

Did that mean he'd thought about remarrying, having more children? Because, according to the rumor mill, he hadn't had a single date since moving to Joyous, despite several attempts to fix him up. Ronnie blinked suddenly. Did *this* count as a date?

"Are you close to your brothers?" he asked.

"Closer than I want to be," she said, softening the words with a smile. "I adore them, but they can be a little…suffocating. Sometimes I want to rebel, shake things up so people see me as more than just Danny and Dev's kid sister."

Though Jason knew she was speaking figuratively, he couldn't imagine how anyone in their right mind could look at the redhead across the table and see a "kid" anything. The white shorts she was wearing today made her legs appear endless, even though she was average height. Granted, he'd been preoccupied with other matters, but how had he not noticed before today how pretty Ronnie was? Maybe he'd started to realize when he'd glimpsed her the other night; that would explain that small, subconscious tug he'd felt before his attention had reverted to Coach Hanover.

Her meadow-green eyes were clear and guileless. While Isobel had always had that mysterious Mona Lisa smile inscrutability, Ronnie's emotions passed over her face in rapid and unapologetic succession—from blushing, to lips pursed in annoyance when she mentioned her brothers' smothering tendencies to laughing out loud if something funny went through her mind. Jason was charmed.

"Thank you for asking me to lunch," he told her. "I'm having fun."

Fun. It wasn't a word he often applied to himself, which was ironic. As a dad, he understood learning through play, understood celebrating the tiny, day-to-day joys with

Emily—sitting in the backyard blowing iridescent soap bubbles together, tickling her just to hear her laugh. So why wasn't he doing more to set that example for his kid, seeking out and appreciating simple pleasures in his own life?

"I'm having a good time, too," Ronnie said.

She leaned closer, as if about to confide a secret, and the increased proximity made him suddenly curious what she smelled like. If there weren't a table between them, would he catch the fragrance of heady perfume or fruity shampoo? He pushed away the nonsensical musings to focus on what she was saying.

"To tell you the truth," she said softly, "I was trying to work up the nerve to approach you the other night. To ask you to dance."

"At Guthrie's? I saw you there." And like an idiot, he'd insisted to Hank that it was time to go, missing an opportunity to discover her scent, to find out how she felt in his arms. "It's been a long time, but I like dancing. Isobel always…"

"Yes?" Ronnie prompted gently.

"That's post-divorce rookie-mistake number one, isn't it? Talking about your ex on a date?"

"I don't mind, I want to hear about your life." She straightened abruptly. "So this is a date?"

He was at a loss for the right thing to say. On the one hand, maybe she hadn't intended the invitation that way, in which case calling it a date would be embarrassing. But given her admission that she'd wanted to ask him to dance, surely she had some interest in him? Jason couldn't help it, he started laughing.

"I feel ridiculous. I'm really out of practice."

Her forehead had puckered into frown lines when he

started chuckling, but her expression smoothed as soon as she realized he wasn't laughing at her. The smile she gave him was understanding and a touch self-deprecating. "Would it make you feel better if I told you I'd never been 'in' practice much to begin with?"

"I find that very hard to believe." He stared into her eyes. Relatively speaking, he was still a newcomer to town, but how could the men who'd known her longer possibly have overlooked her allure? The more he studied her, the stupider he felt for not seeing it sooner himself.

The temperature between them rose a few degrees. Her cheeks pinkened, but she didn't look away. For a moment, he wasn't a harried single father or a mourning grandson, just a healthy male experiencing basic, undiluted arousal for a beautiful woman showing some interest in him. It was intoxicating, liberating—he felt ten years younger.

The sudden sizzling sound seemed strangely appropriate, and he turned to find a man from the kitchen balancing several hot plates on a long oven mitt that extended up past the man's elbow. "Is there anything else I can get you?" the man asked politely.

"No, this looks great," Ronnie said quickly, as if she were eager to get rid of the guy and just be alone with Jason again, in that bubble of silent but mutual attraction.

Or maybe he was projecting his own feelings.

Before he'd had a chance to take the first bite of his food, his cell phone jangled and he pulled it from his pocket with an apologetic glance toward Ronnie. It was probably bad restaurant etiquette to take the call, but the display flashed Spencer, Home. Shouldn't Wanda and the girls be at their movie?

"Hello?"

"Hey, Jason, it's Wanda."

"Everything okay?" It was ridiculous how many implausible worst-case scenarios could go through a parent's head in the span of a second.

"Yeah, but unfortunately my idea to take the kids to the movies this morning was so good that everyone else had it, too. The show sold out before we could get our tickets."

King Cinema, the town theater, had only two screens and extremely limited seating.

"The girls are really disappointed," Wanda continued. "I would take them to this afternoon's showing, but Zoë has a rehearsal for her spring ballet recital. Emily's getting a little fussy, asking for you."

"Should I come get her now?" he asked, his stomach nearly growling in protest. The food smelled wonderful. And, selfishly, he didn't want to give up Ronnie's company.

"I hate for you to rush through your errands. I can keep them entertained a bit longer, but I thought you should know the plans have changed slightly."

Guilt prickled at him. His errands—right. Wanda had offered a precious few hours of free child care because he had a lot of work ahead of him to provide Emily a safe and cheery home environment. Yet he'd blown off his responsibilities in favor of sitting here lusting after a redhead who didn't seem to realize how truly captivating she was.

"I, ah, actually stopped for lunch," he admitted to Wanda. "But I'll come get Em as soon as I'm done. Tell her I'll take her to see the movie soon, that might cheer her up." Before he disconnected the call, he thanked Wanda again for her help. Then he slid the slim phone back in his pocket.

"I take it that was about your little girl?"

"Her plans for the afternoon fell through, and I don'*t* think she's coping with the disappointment well."

Ronnie tilted her head, considering. "Understandable I'd say. After all, I know a lot of adults who hate when thing*s* don't go their way, and she's just a kid who's already had t*o* cope with a lot. How's she holding up since Sophie passed?"

Jason was touched that she'd asked. "It's hard for me t*o* gauge, to get perspective. When it's her and me, she ca*n* be chatty and affectionate, but she's more reserved wit*h* other people. Which could be age-related or mean tha*t* shyness is part of her personality or…maybe, on som*e* level, she's sensitive about letting people in."

"That would be understandable, too. But kids are resilient."

"How old were you when your mom died?"

"Thirteen." She looked away for just a moment. "She'*d* been sick for two years. In a sad way, it's like we lost he*r* by degrees, but the silver lining was that we had time t*o* say our goodbyes. And when she was gone, at least w*e* knew she wasn't suffering anymore."

"My wife was suffering," he heard himself say.

Ronnie looked at him, not saying anything, merel*y* inviting him to speak. Should he? He felt as if he'd alread*y* flunked Dating: A Reintroduction to the Basics by castin*g* an inappropriate pall over lunch instead of keeping it ligh*t* and carefree. But he *wasn't* free of cares…he was respon*-* sible for the well-being of a beautiful little girl, and some*-* times that was hard to shoulder alone.

"Not suffering a physical ailment," he clarified, "but emo*-* tional illness. Isobel had always possessed an, I don't kno*w* ethereal quality. It translated beautifully in her music."

"She was a musician?"

"Cellist. We met as section leaders at a fine arts summer program for kids. She talked about wanting children of her own. After Em was born, though, Isobel became moodier and more fragile than ever. She was falling apart in front of my eyes, and there didn't seem to be a damn thing I could do. The horrible part is, after she left, in some ways it was…"

"A relief?" Ronnie asked, her voice barely a whisper.

His gaze shot up, searching her face. He hadn't been able to bring himself to say the words but he nodded, startled by her perceptiveness. Perhaps she'd experienced similar emotions.

He shoved a hand through his hair. "Emily's only just now reaching the age where I'm starting to see her wonder. She hasn't asked point blank why she doesn't have a mommy—she probably doesn't remember Isobel much—but I see it on the tip of her tongue when she comes home from Zoë's house, when she plays with her dolls. Eventually she's going to ask why her mother left." His deepest fear was that somewhere down the road, she'd blame herself for Isobel's leaving.

"Tough questions," Ronnie said sympathetically. "I don't envy the daily tightrope walk parenting must be."

"A tightrope walk across a lava pit. Full of sharks."

Her green eyes lit with an amusement that warmed him like sunshine. "These would be specially evolved lava-sharks?"

"Naturally." He grinned, feeling better. Still, as much as he would love to spend another couple of hours talking to her, laughing with her, just watching her smile, it seemed wrong to linger over lunch when Wanda was saddled with his cranky daughter. He looked longingly at his barely

touched food. "Ronnie, would it make me the worst lunc
date ever if I asked for to-go boxes?"

"No." Her smile was rueful. "It would just make you
dad."

THE ENTICING AROMA OF peppers and beef emanated from
the warm box in her lap, but the truth was, Ronnie wasn'
all that hungry. Her appetite had been lost in a maelstrom
of other sensations, both physical and emotional, during
her surprising lunch with Jason. From the seat next to him
she stole a glance at his profile. She was awestruck over
the way he'd opened up to her.

Devin, who liked to pretend real emotions didn't exist
could learn a thing or two from Jason.

"You're being terrific about this," Jason said as he
steered his car back into the lot of the hardware store. "I'm
sorry about cutting lunch short."

"You could always make it up to me," she said. *Where
the devil did that come from?* She'd intended to tell him
that it was no problem, but maybe she should brazen ou
her impulsive comment. Look how far her spontaneous
lunch invitation had taken her.

He shifted gears into Park. "Did you have something
specific in mind?"

"Well, since we had to end this date prematurely—"

"I should ask you out on another date." He turned
toward her, a slow grin spreading across his face.
"Veronica, would you like to accompany me to Sprin
Fling?"

Whoa, this "make your own destiny" stuff really
worked. "Spring what?"

"There's a high school dance next weekend, our Spring Fling. I'm actually one of the chaperones."

How many times during her own high school years had she hoped a cute boy would ask her out? But she'd been too shy to convey interest to any of them, and Devin had usually seen it as his job to put the fear of God into anyone who looked twice at her. She'd gone to her prom, but with a group of male and female friends, not someone special.

Someone special.

She met Jason's gray eyes, her knees suddenly so weak that she was grateful to be sitting down. "Are you sure it's okay for a chaperone to bring a date?"

"Trust me, I have Principal Schonrock's express permission."

She wasn't sure exactly what he meant by that, but it wasn't important. "I'd love to go with you."

He promised to get in touch with her later in the week to finalize the details, and she nodded, only hearing every fourth word. She felt as if she were in a fog. *I have a date with Jason McDeere?* Shockingly, she wasn't as nervous as she would have predicted…not that she could have predicted this turn of events. Instead, what she felt was giddy with the anticipation of seeing him again soon.

As she climbed into her own car, she experienced the two universal thoughts shared by girls asked to high school dances: *what will I wear?* and *I can't wait to tell my best friend!*

Chapter Five

"I heard everything, I'm just not sure it sunk in." Lola Ann stood at the kitchen island, theoretically on salad duty. The colander full of washed vegetables and nearby cutting board had been forgotten as Ronnie talked. "You have a date next Saturday with Jason, the guy you once hit with a shopping cart? The guy who makes you stutter when you see him across the lobby at the bank? I know you said you were going to make some changes, but…"

That was the funny part. On some level, she'd thought attracting a guy like Jason would require major changes, like that movie *Sabrina*, where the heroine has to go clear to France to acquire polish and fashion expertise. But Ronnie hadn't needed Lola Ann to help her with her hair or Treble to rehearse being witty; mostly, all she'd needed was the guts to go after what she wanted.

Which didn't mean she'd turn her friends down if they offered to help with wardrobe and hair for the big date.

The back door opened with a bang—Devin had pushed too hard while dragging in two bags of laundry and a paper sack with the local bakery logo on it.

"Don't worry," he told Ronnie, "I didn't bring the clothes for you to wash. I'll take care of it."

"Well, it's just been a day of miracles," she drawled.

"*And* I brought dessert," he added, looking smug. Once we'd hauled everything inside and shut the door behind him, he turned to her with an uncharacteristically earnest expression. "You don't need to worry about us guys, Red. I know we let you pick up a lot of the slack. I think we even figured you liked doing it, that fussing over us was your way of coping. But you shouldn't have to take care of us. You're the baby of the family, *we* should have been doing a better job taking care of *you*."

Ronnie was stunned by the apology. "Dev…"

Lola Ann ducked her head and began chopping carrots, giving them as much privacy as possible for their brother-sister moment. Still, Ronnie caught the sidelong this-is-why-I-like-him glance her friend shot her.

Ronnie hugged her brother, who tolerated the blatant show of affection for a few seconds before disappearing with his clothes into the laundry room. When he reappeared, he boosted himself up onto the kitchen counter next to the bakery bag.

"While I was picking up the cake for tonight," he said, "I ran into Tami Baker."

Frowning, Ronnie tried to place a face with the name she recognized. "You dated her for like a day and a half last spring, right?"

"She's a waitress at Tennessee Tacos now."

Well, that was fast. Ronnie sighed inwardly. "What a coincidence, I was just there today. Food's pretty good."

"Tami said you didn't eat much. Came in with McDeere, sat there for an intense few minutes oblivious to the rest of the world, then boxed up your food to go."

"What, was she standing in the corner taking notes?"

Lola Ann snorted.

Devin overlooked the sarcasm. "First Kaitlyn pointing out your interest in the guy, you threatening us with bodily harm if we so much as talked to him, and now today. How serious is this thing with McDeere?"

"There's no—wait, are we using *your* definition of serious?"

He looked mildly alarmed. "What do you mean 'my definition?'"

"Anything that lasts longer than an hour," she said with saccharine sweetness.

Another snort from Lola Ann, followed by more chopping.

"Now, that was just snippy," Devin admonished as he hopped down from the counter.

Ronnie put her hands on her hips. "But partly true. If you're allowed to worry about my social life, I'm allowed to worry about yours. You don't change your ways, you'll alienate half the women in the state."

He opened the refrigerator. "That's crazy, women love me. Where's the tea?"

"We're out. Tell you what, *you* can brew more since you've decided to be all enlightened and helpful."

"Sure, but we're not done talking about McDeere."

"Actually, we are." Ronnie pulled open the silverware drawer, grabbed a handful of utensils without looking to see what she had, then strode toward the dining room.

As she began setting the table, she heard Devin ask in the other room, "What's gotten into my sister today?"

Lola Ann laughed, but her tone was full of admiration. "She's making some changes."

Ronnie paused, a grin tugging at the corner of her mouth. *Damn right I am.*

"THANKS FOR SUPPER," KAITLYN said graciously. "I feel bad that I couldn't get over in time to help." She'd originally offered to assist with the cooking but had been held up this afternoon with Ashley's troop, working on a float for an upcoming parade.

Ronnie smiled across the table at her sister-in-law. "Well, at least you brought the wine—that probably helped wash the casserole down. Sorry the noodles were so rubbery, and I have no idea what went wrong with the pork."

"I thought that was chicken," Devin said to no one in particular.

"At least we have a great dessert awaiting us," Ronnie said.

"You baked?" Danny asked incredulously.

"No, actually, Dev took care of the cake."

Danny's head swung toward his brother. "*You* baked?"

"Dude, don't be ridiculous. I purchased."

Ashley popped out of her chair to help clear dishes from the table. "Well, *I* thought dinner tasted good, Aunt Ronnie. It wasn't any worse than that eggplant stuff Mama made us eat last week."

Danny chortled, earning a smack across the shoulder from his wife.

Ronnie leaned down toward the little girl. "You know

you're my favorite niece, right?" She could say so without guilt since her brother Will had boys.

"I know." Ashley beamed. Then her expression turned sly. "But it's been too long since we did something 'just us.'"

Ah, suddenly Ashley's cooking compliments and willingness to clean up without being asked were making more sense.

Ronnie set some plates in the sink. "You want me to ask your mom and dad if you can spend the night? We could microwave some popcorn, watch a Disney movie and maybe play poker with Grandpa Wayne later."

"Actually there's a movie out right now I want to see. In the theater. Daddy and Mama both said they were too tired to take me tonight, but I bet they wouldn't mind if *you* wanted to take me."

Ronnie laughed. "I'll see what I can do." The truth was, she loved being cool Aunt Ronnie. *Might be my only real chance at* being *cool.* Over her shoulder, she called, "Who wants cake?"

There were unanimous requests for dessert, and Lola Ann came into the kitchen to help Ronnie scoop ice cream. Ashley carried each plate into the next room, not only using both hands but employing a death grip and walking so slowly Ronnie figured the ice cream would melt by the time it got to the table.

Lola Ann watched in amusement. "She's certainly being careful."

"She's on extra good behavior because she's trying to butter me up."

"Asking for a pony again?"

Ronnie laughed—her niece was mad for horses. "No, thankfully this was a smaller request. Just a movie."

Lola Ann nudged her with her elbow. "You're getting all kinds of date offers today, aren't you?"

"Aunt Ronnie, are you dating someone?"

Sorry, Lola Ann mouthed, even though it was clear she was trying not to laugh.

Both women turned to see Ashley listening avidly, her head cocked to the side as she waited for their answer. Yet she didn't give them a chance to respond. "My friend Melanie, her parents got divorced, and she says her mom is dating. If her mom gets married again, Melanie gets to be the flower girl at the wedding. Could I be your flower girl?"

"Uh…honey, I'm not really dating anyone, per se. We don't need to worry about weddings. Why don't you go take this piece to your dad?"

"'Kay."

Lola Ann waited until the girl was gone again before giggling. "Really, you should make Ashley a junior bridesmaid. Emily would be the flower girl."

"Oh, you're a big help."

But Ronnie's mock-glare only made Lola Ann giggle harder. "S-sorry. I think the wine's gone to my head."

"You've only had a glass and a half!"

"Yeah, but I was caught up reading this historical novel today and missed lunch, then there was dinner." Though Lola Ann had gamely tried a few bites, she apparently had more discerning palate than the men in Ronnie's family, who'd had years of practice choking down her cooking.

They dished up the rest of the cake and ice cream. As

Ronnie was placing the carton of Vanilla back in the freezer she realized her niece had never returned for more plates

"Ashley?"

The girl came skipping into the room. "What's 'tact'?'

"It's when you try to tell someone the truth withou hurting their feelings, I guess. Why?"

"I went to ask Daddy what 'per se' meant and told him about how you're not dating and then he and Mama starter talking about someone named Jason who has a deer and she told Uncle Dev he needs to learn tact. I thought mayb it was like math or something."

Lola Ann was bent over the kitchen island, her shoul ders shaking with silent mirth.

Ronnie groaned but bravely carried two plates into the next room. "So…what's new in world politics?"

"Same old, same old," Danny said. "The real questio is, what's new with *you?*"

She played dumb. "My house, as of Wednesday. Yo still available to help me move the pieces of furniture?"

From the head of the table, Wayne Carter answered, "O course he is, darlin'. That's one of the advantages of workin for your old man. I can close shop for the afternoon and we'l have you all moved in before supper. But I think what you brother really wanted to hear about is this new beau of yours.

"I don't think having lunch with a guy qualifies him a a 'beau,' Dad."

"Then you aren't seeing him again?" Kaitlyn sounde disappointed.

"Well…it's a small town. I'm sure I'll see him. Aroun Sometime." Next Saturday, for instance.

Devin guffawed. "You're turning that shade of red you always get when you're trying to lie."

"Aunt Ronnie would never lie," Ashley said loyally around a mouthful of fudge devil's food cake.

"We're interested in your life," Wayne said patiently, "and the people in it, because we love you."

"You do have a track record of questionable romantic choices," Danny said. "We can't help wanting to look out for you."

"*What* questionable choices?"

"Ralphie Goodling, our former next-door neighbor who tried to woo you by burping the alphabet."

"I was seven, you cretin!" Although, if memory served, she *had* been impressed; Ralphie had been the only guy she'd ever heard belch more impressively than her brothers. But he'd moved to Kentucky when she was ten, so theirs was a love not meant to be.

"How do you burp the alphabet?" Ashley asked, sounding fascinated.

"Never you mind," her father told her. "It's just something gross boys do."

Devin picked up where Danny had left off. "Ronnie, you have great taste in friends." He nodded toward Lola Ann, who smiled shyly and took a nervous sip from her wineglass. "But when it comes to guys... Case in point, Grayson Jones, your sophomore year. You would have gone to Homecoming with that jerk if—"

"If what?" Ronnie demanded. Grayson had broken off their date a few days beforehand, mumbling about a speeding ticket and getting grounded. She'd been crushed.

At the time, she'd thought he was the best-looking guy she'd ever seen.

Of course, that was years before she'd met Jason McDeere

Danny and Devin exchanged sheepish glances, bu neither of them would meet her gaze.

"I knew it!" Ronnie tossed her napkin down on the table "You guys did something to scare him away, didn't you?"

"We just had a little chat with him," Danny said. "He was a sleaze. All he cared about was getting his date behind the stadium bleachers and then bragging about i at school."

Kaitlyn jabbed her husband in the ribs, muttering abou "little pitchers."

Turning toward her niece, Ronnie said, "Ashley, honey why don't you go in the kitchen and look for the newspa per so we can check tonight's movie time?"

Once the girl had scampered off, Ronnie's glare ping ponged between her brothers, Devin sitting on her side of the table, Danny opposite. "There's no point in my telling you what high-handed asses you were back then because it's in the past. But I am a grown woman now so you're just going to have to trust me to make the bes decisions for me."

"That's right!" Lola Ann nodded in emphatic support probably feeling guilty for laughing at her so much earlie "Ronnie's intelligent and capable, and Jason's a great guy I bet you couldn't find anyone in town with a bad word to say about him. Besides, there comes a time in a girl's lif when she needs a little behind-the-bleachers action."

Wayne choked on his cake, Danny's lips twitched as h

ried not to grin, and Devin's jaw dropped. Even Lola Ann erself looked startled.

"Ah, that's not exactly what I was going to say," Ronnie queaked, stealing a glance at her dad, "but thanks."

Lola Ann was now blushing almost impressively nough to rival Ronnie, but her voice was level. "Anytime."

HE MOVIE THEATER WAS CROWDED—not surprising since the nly three Saturday night hotspots were the cinema, Guthrie's nd a bowling alley. Rather than try to step over people to ind places in the long center rows, Ronnie steered her niece oward the four-seat side row closest to the entrance ramp. 'revious outings with Ashley had taught her that the little girl vould need to use the restroom at least once. This way, they ad quick exit access and there was no chance of someone aller than Ashley sitting right in front of her.

"Thanks for bringing me, Aunt Ronnie! I always have he most fun with you."

Even if Ronnie had been something of a tomboy at Ashley's age, she was more prone to enjoy the animated rincess movie than her big brother. Of course, she sus-ected part of Ashley's joy stemmed from Ronnie's inabil-:y to say no at the concession stand. Probably the popcorn *nd* sour gummies were overkill after the cake back home. 'hen again, Ronnie had grabbed her niece and the excuse > flee an increasingly awkward conversation, so neither f them had actually finished their dessert.

"I'm glad we're here, too," Ronnie said.

Ashley situated herself in her chair, hefting her soda into ie cup holder. As the overhead lights dimmed, Ronnie pened the candies and dumped them into the popcorn—

all the better to experience the sweet-sour-salty combina
tion. Midway through the first preview, a man holding a
little girl's hand appeared in the aisle.

"Excuse me," he said, trying to duck down so that he
wasn't in anyone's way. "Are those seats—Ronnie?"

Even in the semidarkness, the smile Jason gave her was
far more heady than the half glass of wine she'd had earlier.

"Hi. The, uh, the seats are completely free. Ashley, why
don't we scoot down so that Mr. McDeere and his daughter
don't have to step over us."

Recognition lit Ashley's features. "You're Jason with a
deer!"

He raised an eyebrow. "I suppose that might be me."

"My mom and—"

"Ashley, honey, more scooting. Less talking."

Emily sat next to Ronnie, leaving the aisle seat for
Jason. "Hello," the little girl said solemnly. She was
wearing a green T-shirt that featured an embroidered but
terfly, pants that seemed a smidge too short and a rhine
stone tiara that was missing a few jewels. She barely
weighed enough to hold the seat down.

"I like your princess crown," Ronnie whispered.

Emily twisted the hem of her shirt. "I wanna be
pwincess when I get big."

Jason laid his big hand over his daughter's. "You already
are, sweet pea."

"Uh-uh." She gave him the long-suffering look of a
child tolerating a slow-witted parent; Ronnie had seen
the look on Ashley's face before. "We don't have a
castle, Daddy."

He chuckled at his daughter's literalism. "Guess I can't argue with that."

The movie started soon after, but Ronnie couldn't focus on the screen. She was too tempted to sneak peeks at Jason's chiseled profile in the semidarkness. Once, when she stole a sidelong glance in his direction, she caught him doing the same. Her face immediately heated. For a long time after, she kept her eyes straightforward.

Ashley and Emily, despite their difference in age, laughed at most of the same places in the movie. The first time Ronnie heard the toddler's deep belly laugh, she was startled, then amused. It was a big sound for such a little girl. She knew twenty minutes in the kid's company didn't qualify her as a child therapist, but she wanted to believe that Emily would weather life's storms just fine. Despite her first shy hello, she seemed to have a natural exuberance lurking just beneath the surface.

As the movie wore on, Ronnie found it more and more difficult to focus on the storyline and the myriad of musical numbers. Instead, all her senses kept returning to Jason McDeere and the unexpected intimacy of sitting close to him in a dark theater. *Along with two little girls. At a G-rated movie.* It was hardly a sexy situation, she reminded her buzzing hormones. During the second half of the show, her awareness of him only heightened. He sat with his arm casually draped over the back of his daughter's chair and once brushed Ronnie's shoulder when she swiveled to find a more comfortable position. At the mere feel of his fingers on her skin, she jumped as though she were watching a horror movie.

"Sorry," Jason murmured.

He was instantly shushed by both girls, prompting exchanged glances of amusement between him and Ronnie.

When the movie ended, the house lights came on. Ronnie felt comically exposed, sitting there with the huge tub of popcorn that she and Ashley had shared. Either Jason didn't believe in feeding his daughter junk food, or they hadn't taken the time for snacks because they'd almost missed the beginning of the movie. She stood, brushing a stray kernel from the front of her shirt. Though she hadn't thought much about it in the dim lighting, she wasn't what one could call glamorously dressed. Not that King Cinema required glamour, but it might be nice if just once she could run into Jason while she was wearing a skirt and makeup.

Next Saturday, she promised herself. She'd find a dress this week to knock his socks off.

Emily began bouncing up and down. "Ice cream! Ice cream!"

"All right," Jason conceded with a smile. He looked toward Ronnie. "Emily's only been to a couple of movies, but we've always capped off the outing with a trip to Blacky's."

"Yummy," Ashley declared, peering around her aunt to get a better look at Jason.

"I don't suppose the two of you would like to join us?" he asked.

Ashley whooped with delight. "Yes! Can we, Aunt Ronnie? Pleeeeease."

Ronnie bit her lower lip; she was tempted to parrot her niece's exuberance, but technically she and Ashley had hit their threshold for sweets. Then she suddenly realized that Jason's shoulders had tensed. She doubted he was even aware of it, but his posture had grown more rigid since he issued the invitation. Was he nervous?

The possibility was so endearing that she heard herself reply, "We'd love to. Meet you there?"

Once she and Ashley were safely buckled into her car, Ronnie captured her niece's gaze in the rearview mirror, "Don't even *think* about ordering a double scoop. And the next time we have a girls' night out, it's going to include lots of healthy vegetables!"

The eight-year-old giggled. "Whatever you say, Aunt Ronnie."

JASON WANTED TO HOLD THE DOOR open for Ronnie, but since his daughter shot into Blacky's Emporium like a cannonball with a sweet tooth, he hurried after Emily instead. Though he doubted any real danger lurked inside, he stayed close to her in crowds. Business was thriving, and many of the booths and tall two-seater tables were already occupied. White-haired grandparents shared sundaes with their grandchildren, teenagers clearly on a date stared into each other's eyes while their neglected milkshakes melted, and Berta Feeney, a science teacher from the high school, sat in a horseshoe-shaped booth with her husband and three sons.

Jason had scooped Emily up in his arms so she couldn't run off, and waited for Ronnie and Ashley to reach his side before approaching the counter. As soon as he'd asked her to join them, he'd second-guessed himself. He'd greatly enjoyed their lunch together and was, for the first time since agreeing to chaperone, truly looking forward to the Spring Fling. Yet dipping his toe back in the dating pool was nerve-racking enough when it was just two adults involved—was it wrong to add Emily to the mix so soon?

Then again, they were certainly a package deal. Besides Ronnie was out with her niece, which kept this outing casual and made her even more appealing in his eyes. She seemed good with kids.

Jason ordered first, getting a waffle cone packed with banana-pudding ice cream, complete with marshmallows and bits of vanilla cookies, and a small bowl of bubble-gum ice cream. Or, as Emily called it, "the pink kind." Then he told the girl behind the counter, "And whatever they're having, too."

"Rainbow sherbet in a sugar cone," Ashley said over top of Ronnie's protests about paying.

"I can't let you get this," Ronnie was arguing. "You bought lunch."

"So next time we go somewhere, you can pick up the tab," he said, proud of how matter-of-factly the words came out. As if dining out with women was simply a part of life when the truth was, he usually only ate meals with the very short female whose food he had to cut.

Ronnie's smile was dazzling. "I'll have to take you up on that."

Lord, he hoped so. He doubted she had any idea how much he would look forward to an invitation from her. For the past year, he'd been so busy—making lesson plans, trying to get through a school day with enough energy left to spend quality time with Em, working on Gran's house and yard—that he'd been *existing* more than living. Just coping wasn't enough anymore. He didn't want to "get by." He wanted to wake up in the morning anticipating life, smiling at what the day might bring.

When Ronnie added her drink to the order, Jason turned

to her in surprise. "Just a beverage? You can't come to the ice cream Emporium and not get dessert!"

"You can if you've scarfed down a tub of popcorn." Her smile was self-conscious as she pressed a hand to her flat stomach.

Surely she wasn't worried about the extra calories? He ran his gaze down her slim figure, his body responding in primitive approval. The gentle flare of her hips and those long, long legs. She had on denim capris now, but the image of her in the white shorts from earlier was indelibly stamped on his mind.

"Aunt Ronnie's favorite is mint-chocolate," Ashley chimed in. "You should get her that."

"Ash." Ronnie's reprimand was halfhearted, at best. She'd brightened at the mention of her favorite flavor.

"We'll take another waffle cone with mint-chocolate," Jason told the uniformed girl behind the counter.

She grinned, punching the appropriate buttons. "Sure thing." As he carried Emily over to the napkin dispenser to stock up, he heard the Emporium employee confide to Ronnie, "Wish *my* boyfriend tried to feed me extra ice cream. He's always dropping hints that I'd look better if I went on a diet."

Ronnie clucked her tongue, sounding amusingly maternal as she scolded, "You're lovely. Don't you dare let some boy talk you into becoming a twig!"

The four of them found a booth, pairing off with an adult and child on each side. Though the seating arrangement made perfect sense, especially given the mess he knew Emily would make, Jason couldn't help wishing he'd been sitting next to Ronnie. Then again, perhaps the extra nearness would prove too torturous. As it was, he had to avoid the temptation to stare as she licked her ice cream, catching a few melted drops at the corner of her mouth with her tongue.

"Jason?" A woman's inquisitive voice distracted him from his irrational jealousy of mint-chocolate ice cream. "I thought that was you."

"Hi, Berta." He smiled at the other teacher. "Ronnie, do you know Berta Feeney?"

"Oh, Ronnie and I go way back. She resurrected the 'bargain' sports car my husband bought during his mid-life crisis." Berta's friendly expression didn't mask her blatant curiosity.

While it wasn't exactly front-page news worthy of the *Joyous Journal-Report* that he was having ice cream with a woman, Jason knew that his not dating anyone since moving to town had been noticed—and, if Principal Schonrock were to be believed, lamented. It occurred to him for the first time that, after he took Ronnie to the dance, people would talk about them, link them as a couple. He took a moment to turn it over in his mind and discovered that, for a man who'd been so uninterested in dating, he was surprisingly comfortable with that idea.

Something about Ronnie put him at ease, even while she simultaneously made him feel like a guy with his first crush.

"Well." Berta glanced over her shoulder. "I have to go drag my crew away from the air-hockey table. We leave tomorrow for a camping trip."

"Have fun," Ronnie told her. "When I was young, we went camping all the time. Although, to be honest, trying o stay alert for my brothers' pranks didn't make me a camping enthusiast."

Berta pulled a face. "I'm not one, either—bugs, sleeping on the ground and the latrines? By the time spring break ends, I'll be desperate to get back to work! See you next week, Jason."

"Bye, Berta."

Emily, who had plowed through the first half of her ice cream and was now stirring what was left around the bowl in pink swirls, looked up at him. "What's a 'trine?"

"A latrine is a bathroom," Ashley said, obviously excited that she knew the answer. "We have them at horse camp."

"Oh." Then Emily's eyes widened, the mention of restrooms triggering a belated realization in his nearly potty-trained daughter. "Need to go pee-pee!"

"You want me to take her?" Ronnie offered before popping the last bite of waffle cone into her mouth.

Jason looked forward to the day Emily could use the restroom without assistance and he could simply wait outside in view of the door; in the meantime, he usually had to bring her into the men's restroom. "That would be great, if she doesn't mind going with you." It normally took Em some time to warm up to strangers.

But either Emily seriously approved of his choice in women or her need to go had temporarily overruled any inherent shyness, because she scrambled over her father, her hand extended toward Ronnie.

"What about you?" Ronnie asked her niece. "Want to come with us?"

"Hurry," Emily urged as Ashley shook her head.

"Okay." Ronnie lifted Emily and carried her to the back of the Emporium.

He couldn't help but watch them. It was such a simple thing, but beautiful, Em's dark head close to Ronnie's bright red hair. As they disappeared through the crowd, he heard the unmistakable bellow of his daughter's laugh and a lower answering chuckle, and he lost his breath, the strangest feeling blooming in his chest. He hadn't felt it very much since Gran died, and it took him a moment to place the emotion: hope.

Chapter Six

By the time the keys to her new house were handed over Wednesday afternoon, Ronnie's cramped fingers hurt from signing and initialing document after document. And her face hurt from smiling so much. Mere hours later, the rest of her body had caught up—she ached in muscles she hadn't even realized existed.

"I take back every mean thing I ever said about either of you," she called as Danny and Devin maneuvered her queen-size mattress down the hall. "Thank you, you're both princes among men."

Her belongings hadn't seemed to amount to much when scattered throughout her much larger childhood home. But as they'd loaded them up to drive to this section of Joyous, she swore they had multiplied. The guys had told her they'd carry stuff in while she worked in the living room. Her very first job, begun immediately, was cutting and ripping out the horrendously ugly shag carpet some genius had put in the living room. She had boxes of faux-hardwood laminate flooring she was going to install over the concrete slab.

Devin had commented that there was no point to filling the room with furniture she'd just have to move out of the room in order to tackle the floors. So they were taking care of the heavy lifting, she was divesting her beloved new home of the shag atrocity and Lola Ann had said she'd come over later to help with odds and ends such as lining the cabinets and drawers with shelving paper before they unpacked Ronnie's dishes.

Ronnie got about a quarter of the floor covered before she had to go to the garage and cut more panels to fit correctly. She was using a power saw when Lola Ann parked in the driveway.

Her friend chuckled. "Now, see, I wouldn't know how to use one of those even if I did own one."

"You'd just check out a book on electric tools and teach yourself."

"I notice there are still some boxes in the back of your car. You want me to start unloading those, or is there something else I should help with first?"

"Well…" Ronnie grinned, lowering her voice. "Devin looked pretty hot and sweaty last time I saw him. You could always offer him a glass of lemonade."

Lola Ann darted a nervous glance to the front door, which was opening. "Ronnie, shh!"

"Looks like you can take a librarian out of the library," drawled Devin from the porch, "but you can't make her stop shushing people."

Turning toward him, Lola Ann made a show of rolling her eyes. "Remind me again how you get women to go out with you?"

He smirked. "I have certain talents."

Lola Ann's eyes widened, then she spun on her heel toward Ronnie's car. Which meant that she didn't see the way Dev's gaze followed her or that his teasing expression dropped from his face once her back was turned. Ronnie glanced from her brother to her best friend, eyebrows raised.

Interesting.

THE GUYS HAD LEFT AND Lola Ann and Ronnie sat on the floor of the new kitchen, eating delivery pizza straight out of the cardboard box.

"Maybe I don't actually need to use plates," Ronnie mused. "Think of all the dish-washing it'll save me."

"There's a mature attitude," Lola Ann scoffed.

Without warning, Ronnie flashed back to the day she'd learned, as a twelve-year-old, that Sue Carter had no chance of winning her fight against cancer. In some ways, Ronnie had matured to an old soul that day, at a time when her friends' biggest concerns were which teacher they'd get for middle-school homeroom and whether they were ever going to get boobs or not. *In my case,* Ronnie thought with a wry glance down, *not.*

"You know what, Lola Ann? I think maybe I'm due a little immaturity."

Lola Ann held up her can of diet soda in a one-sided toast. "Woo-hoo, party at Ronnie's!"

"Actually, that's a good idea. In a week or two, I should have a housewarming party. Invite you and my brothers, Treble and Keith, Bill and Charity. It will be fun!" Excitement pulsed through her. Though she realized that she could have thrown a party whenever she'd wanted at her dad's place, this was different. This was *hers.* She could sleep till noon on the weekends and eat breakfast in her underwear!

"Hey." She nudged Lola Ann's foot with her own. "Speaking of my brothers, what's up with you and Dev?"

"Um, unrequited love on my part, total unawareness on his. Why do you ask?"

"You sure nothing happened Saturday?" About the time Ronnie had been using her niece as an escape hatch, Devin had declared he was headed to Guthrie Hall and Lola Ann had said that sounded good to her, too.

"Well, we rode together in the car and it was…fun. We spend a lot of time together, but I can't think of the last time we were alone like that. I gave him a hard time about his pitiful taste in music. But then when we got there, it was status quo. He started flirting with some woman in a skin-tight top. I mean, we just rode together, it wasn't like he was my date," Lola Ann said morosely.

"He didn't even dance with you?"

"Well sure, twice in two hours. That doesn't mean anything. He dances with *you,* too. Mostly, I danced with Bear. Then on the way back to your dad's so I could pick up my car, Devin was different. Almost cranky. I figure he was upset because taking me back cramped his style. He probably wished he could have gone home with Miss Tight Top."

"Or," Ronnie said slowly, "maybe he didn't like seeing you dance with Bear."

Lola Ann gaped, then let out a high, thin laugh. "Now you're just talking crazy. Forget about my Saturday…it wasn't nearly as promising as your movie night."

Ronnie smiled at the memory. "I admit, I normally have fun with Ash, but that particular evening exceeded expectations. I was half terrified to take Emily to the restroom and leave Ashley alone with Jason. Heaven knows what the kid might say to him."

Lola Ann laughed. "She's always entertaining, though. When she talks to me, I can barely keep up with how fast her mind works. She'll start one sentence, somehow switch topics in the middle, and by the end of it be on something seemingly unrelated."

"I love her dearly, but I'm usually exhausted by the time I deliver her back home." One of the benefits of being an aunt rather than a parent; Ronnie got to do all the fun stuff, then pass the child—and the responsibility—back over to someone else.

"Well, *I'm* exhausted now." Lola Ann rose, stretching. "I should head home."

It wasn't that late, but they'd certainly expended a lot of effort today.

"Thanks for all your help."

Lola Ann reached for her purse on the counter. This house had far less counter space and pantry space than Ronnie's previous residence, but since she didn't plan to spend much time toiling in the kitchen, she didn't care.

"We forgot to test your phone," Lola Ann said suddenly, digging her cell out of the purse.

Ronnie had prearranged to have the new number activated by 5:00 p.m. Since she hadn't been able to find her phone, Lola Ann had called for the pizza. Ronnie had plugged in her cordless about twenty minutes ago and checked for a dial tone.

"Give me the number again," Lola Ann said. "I can program it in and make sure it works before I go."

A minute later, the phone on Ronnie's kitchen wall rang,

and she grinned. "Twenty-five years old and I finally have my own private line."

Once Lola Ann left, Ronnie decided she'd take a hot shower, then go to bed early. But she stood under the luxurious steam far longer than she'd intended, knowing that no one was going to knock on the door, asking her if she would be out soon. By the time she shrugged into the terry-cloth bathrobe she'd hung on a hook outside the stall, she felt reenergized. Not in body, but spirit, far too excited to drop off to sleep.

Stretched across her bed, she stared at the foreign landscape of the surrounding white walls. Was this how artists felt when confronted with the potential of a blank canvas? She could do whatever she wanted to make this place hers—hit garage sales and antique stores for old furniture to refurbish, order sleek contemporary pieces online, explore her heretofore unknown Goth side and paint the whole shebang black… She felt alive with possibility.

Rolling over, she grabbed her phone. Seconds later, she had the number from information for the person she suddenly wanted to share this with. She held her breath as the phone rang, hoping he was home, hoping he answered.

"Hello?"

A thrill raced up her spine. "Jason? It's Ronnie."

"Hi." His voice deepened the tiniest fraction; she might not have even noticed except that she was listening so intently. "Today was the big move, right?"

"Yep." She sat up, bouncing a little on the mattress. "I'm phoning you from my brand-new bedroom! It's not too late to call, is it?"

"No, this is fine. Em's in bed already. Since I'm or

reak this week, I got to spend the day with her at an
utdoor park. She's out like a light. And I was planning to
all you, anyway, to find out what you're wearing."

"Huh?" She glanced down at the robe, feeling a blush
limb her cheeks.

"T-to the dance. It's customary for a date to bring a
orsage, and—"

"Oh. Right, a corsage. Jason, you don't have to do that."
Especially since she didn't have the first clue what she was
wearing! She and Treble were supposed to meet Lola Ann
n front of the library tomorrow and hit some outlet stores
hat Treble swore by. "I'm not really a flower kind of girl.
But it was a nice thought."

He was silent for a long moment, and she wondered if
he'd hurt his feelings. Then he laughingly admitted,
Well, it was my proposed excuse for calling you."

She was absurdly flattered but kept her tone light. "If you
ver need an excuse to *see* me, you can always bring your
ar to the shop and claim to have heard vague rattling noises."

He laughed. "I'll keep that in mind. I'm hoping to see
lot more of you, Ronnie."

She curled her toes and kicked her feet against the mattress
n a small, stationary happy dance. "Really? I'd like that."

"I like *you*. And so does Emily. She was talking about
ou at the park today, wanted to know why you couldn't
ome play with us."

"That's really sweet. Maybe some other time," she said.

It wasn't until after they'd hung up the phone that
Ronnie experienced a frisson of unease. *So does Emily.* On
he one hand, it was great that the little girl liked Ronnie—
he feeling was mutual. But…

Ronnie had been attracted to Jason from the first moment they'd met, but it hadn't been a *real* part of her life. It had been more a pleasant daydream simmering low on a backburner, like when a person fantasizes about how they'd spend the money if they won the lottery, whether they actually played the lottery or not. Because she hadn't, deep down, expected something to come of her one-sided crush—the man hadn't dated in the entire time he'd lived here!—she'd never truly considered the logistics of the potential relationship. On Saturday, she felt like she'd struck gold when he'd not only agreed to have lunch with her but obviously enjoyed her company.

She hadn't thought ahead to whether or not his daughter would like her, too. Or what that would mean. After only one movie and trip for ice cream, Em wanted Ronnie to join them for family excursions to the park.

No big deal. Pushing her in a swing and catching her at the bottom of the slide. I can do that.

But Emily had already lost the two most important women in her life. Ronnie remembered a home ec teacher she'd had her freshman year. Because Ronnie had possibly the least amount of natural aptitude in the entire class, Mrs. Velmer had spent some extra time with her. As a result, Ronnie had begun to imagine a bond that went beyond teacher-student. She'd started visiting Mrs. Velmer's classroom in the morning just for a chat, everything from what her brothers were up to that week to Ronnie's ideas for the school's Name the Mascot contest. After a little while, Mrs. Velmer started to gently drop hints that she had grading and preparation to do in the morning. Eventually, her husband had taken a job transfer and Ronnie's surrogate-mother figure had moved to another school district.

Looking back on it, the poor woman had probably been relieved.

From the brief time Ronnie had spent with Emily, the girl seemed great. But like Mrs. Velmer, years before, Ronnie wasn't sure she was ready to be anyone's surrogate mother.

Jumping the gun a bit, aren't you?

Seriously, what was she worried about? Her abilities as a stepmother? A little presumptuous considering Jason hadn't even kissed her.

Yet. She grinned into the darkness, her worries fading. Hopefully, they could take care of that on Saturday.

THEY'D AGREED JASON SHOULD pick her up at seven-fifteen so that he had a few minutes to see the house before they needed to leave for the dance. By seven-thirteen, Ronnie had changed her earrings three times, checked her teeth for lipstick more times than she could count, and was starting to seriously reconsider leaving her hair down. She was so accustomed to pulling it back that it just seemed…in the way somehow.

When the doorbell let out its discordant gong—she should see if there was something she could do to fix that—relief filled her. She couldn't take any more anticipation. She opened the door, and Jason's eyes went wide.

"Wow. I…wow."

Happiness bloomed in her, along with a newfound confidence. The green halter-top dress was simple but flattering. She'd applied just enough makeup to avoid feeling like a mechanic, and she'd brushed her hair until it shined, pinning up a few strands on one side with a sparkly barrette Ashley had given her for her birthday.

She grinned up at him. "That's quite an impressive vocabulary you have there, Professor."

He looked pretty wow-worthy himself. She studied him, from his incredible eyes to the crisp white shirt he wore unbuttoned at the collar beneath a navy jacket. Although, she had to laugh at the terra-cotta pot he held in one arm. A large yellow bow was tied around the plant.

"I'd hate to see the wristband that goes with *that* corsage," she teased.

His grin was almost bashful. "It's a fern. I wanted to bring you a small housewarming gift. It's nonflowering. And I also got you this." He reached into the pocket of his blazer and brought out a miniature vehicle.

She reached out to take it, enjoying the brief electric moment when their fingers touched and the heady knowledge that there would be many more such moments throughout the evening. Closer inspection of the toy revealed that it was a black monster truck with yellow-and-red flames painted on the sides.

Ronnie burst out laughing. "Thank you. Come on in and I'll give you the ten-cent tour." She set the gifts on the kitchen counter, feeling, for a moment, almost nervous at viewing her new home through someone else's eyes. This was a pretty modest house, and it would take time and effort for her to uncover all its charm, but—

"It's great," he said, walking from the kitchen to the living room. "Nice high ceilings, I bet you get great natural light through these windows during the day. And I love the floors."

Pride swelled within her. "I've been working on the

ooring all week. Next, I'm repainting the hallway and the athroom. There are some minor wiring issues, too, but I eed to go up in the attic for that and Dad's planning to ome by and help."

"You're putting me to shame," he told her. "I've had r longer to work on Gran's house, but my progress is low going."

She gestured toward the sliding glass door. "The ackyard needs a lot of work, but I have some landscap-ng plans for this summer. Through here is the dining oom." Mostly bare except for a small curio cabinet, in which she'd displayed a few of the old Jewel T dishes her randmother had left her.

Jason looked around, and they compared notes on dif-erent window treatments and their mutual dislike for iniblinds.

"Gran kept a clean house, but I swear not even she could eep the dang things free of dust. And Emily's always ending them up when she tries to look outside." He lanced over his shoulder. "She's across the street tonight the Spencers', attempting her very first sleepover with oë. When I dropped her off, she seemed equal parts ervous and excited."

Ronnie knew the feeling.

Jason checked his watch. "We should probably head out oon."

"I'm ready. I think you've seen just about everything. he guest room is full of unpacked boxes, and that just aves my, um, bedroom." Her cheeks heated.

He stepped closer, reaching out to cup the side of her ce. "You're blushing again." Far from the mocking way her brothers used to say it, from Jason, it sounded like an endearment.

Reflexively, she turned her head, leaning into his palm. They stood there, so close together, she fancied she could hear his heartbeat in the quiet house.

"You know, Ronnie, it's been…a long time since I've been on a date. I'm rusty at this."

"You've been doing just fine so far."

He traced his thumb over the arch of her upper lip. "I know it breaks tradition, but would it be wrong to kiss you good-night at the beginning of the date?"

Her pulse pounded, her insides dissolving into liquid heat. She couldn't even form words to reply, merely parted her lips in breathless anticipation and tilted her head, glad for the extra height her shoes provided. Jason looked into her eyes as he moved toward her, a simple but erotic intimacy. His kiss was hesitant at first, just a light brush of lips, exploratory and gentle. The delicate touch elicited a sigh from her.

He returned, more eager and possessive this time. As he'd done earlier with the pad of his thumb, he traced her lip with his tongue, then slipped into her mouth.

Most car engines were powered by a combustion cycle—hundreds of tiny, controlled explosions. That's how Jason's kiss made her feel, as if sparks were igniting throughout her body. She could almost see fireworks behind her closed eyes. But these were definitely not *controlled* sensations. Her limbs quivered, and she tightened her hold on him. He thrust his tongue against hers, then drew back slightly to suck at her bottom lip. Her groan of approval nearly morphed into one of protest when he pulled away.

"Ronnie, I…" His silvery eyes burned brightly.

"Yeah." She felt as if she might never catch her breath again, but in a good way.

With visible reluctance, he dragged his gaze from her face to his watch. "We really should be going."

"Yeah." And *she'd* teased *him* earlier about his limited vocabulary?

But she couldn't think of any appropriate words for what they'd just shared. Except, possibly, *more, please.*

As he opened the car door for her, she asked, "So, even though you gave me my good-night kiss early, do you think I can still get one later?"

For just a second, he leaned his body into hers, his smile wicked. "Count on it."

Chapter Seven

"I think we've scared the young people," Ronnie said in amused undertones.

"'Young people?' You're not exactly ancient," he kidded as they made their way off the dance floor. "And I don't think we alarmed them so much as reduced them to gales of hysterical laughter."

The deejay had gone retro for a few minutes, playing music Jason actually knew, and he'd enjoyed cutting loose on the dance floor. He'd caught more than one of his students giggling in his direction. *Well, I did promise them.* It had been fun, but he hoped the next set included more slow songs. He wanted the excuse to hold Ronnie closer.

Then again, after the incredibly steamy kiss they'd shared back at her house, maybe closer wasn't such a wise idea right now.

Better to push that memory away until later. "Out of curiosity, just how old are you?"

"Twenty-five."

"Oh." At her age, he hadn't even been married. Now here he was, a divorced single father. *Time flies.*

"That's not a problem, is it?" she asked.

"What?" He realized he was frowning and quickly smoothed his expression. "Not at all. I was just thinking that there are a lot of things we don't know about each other."

"I know you turned thirty-three last winter, and Sophie was planning to make you a German chocolate cake, your favorite."

"I'm flattered you paid such close attention."

"Maybe I was," she admitted. "But in all fairness, plenty of other women in Joyous would know the same details. It's a small town. When a good-looking bachelor moves in, his stats are practically published in the *Journal-Report*."

He remembered a few grocery store encounters, women leaning down to coo over how cute Emily was, or neighbors who'd brought over baked goods and casseroles, especially after Gran passed away. He just hadn't been ready…more important, those women just hadn't been Ronnie.

They'd made their way to one of the round tables, decorated simply with a white tablecloth and a handful of glittery confetti. With a grateful sigh, Ronnie sat.

"I should have chosen shoes that were more broken in," she admitted. "I love dancing, but my feet are killing me."

"How about you rest those tired toes," he offered, "and I'll go get us some punch?"

"Sounds perfect."

He turned to go but couldn't resist looking back at her, prompting him to collide with junior track star Wallace Daugherty. Wallace, he was quick to notice, was *also* staring at Ronnie.

"Mr. McDeere." The boy straightened. "So, you're here with the mechanic? A chick who's hot *and* knows about cars? Dude, that's awesome!"

"Don't call Ms. Carter a 'chick,' Wallace. Show some respect." He wondered if he should also chastise Wallace for calling her hot—although she *was,* especially in that green dress. Hard to fault Wallace for being observant. "Stay out of trouble tonight, okay, Wallace?"

"Sure thing, dude. I mean, Mr. McDeere."

Principal Schonrock stood vigil at the refreshment table—making good on her promise to thwart any flask-bearing would-be punch spikers—and she nodded as Jason approached. "You look very dapper." The corner of her mouth twitched as she teased, "Except for maybe on the dance floor. I'm not sure how to describe that."

He grinned. "It's called raising the roof. Don't tell me you and Mr. Schonrock aren't going to dance later?"

"He has a fishing tournament this weekend, so I'm here solo." She nodded toward where Ronnie sat. "I see you aren't here alone, though."

"No, ma'am." He reached for the clear plastic ladle in the punch bowl. "And you were right about this being more fun with a date."

She sniffed. "I'm so often right. I just wish the students realized that more."

He laughed and nodded once more before carrying the glasses back to Ronnie. "You've made the principal very happy."

Ronnie quirked an eyebrow in question.

"She had suggested my bringing a date."

"That seems an odd faculty requirement." Then again, people got away with a little more oddness in small towns.

"Well, she was worried, on account of my rare status as

a single man and, of course, devastating good looks," he said dryly.

She grinned. "They really are devastating."

"Yeah?" His sardonic manner slipped as he met her eyes. He didn't care about his looks, but he did care about what *she* saw when she looked at him. Heartbeats of time passed, slowly becoming measures of music behind him as one song faded into the next. "I have no idea what I was saying."

"That your principal coerced you into asking me out, probably to avoid catfights in the hall between all the teachers who hoped you'd ask one of *them*."

He laughed. "There's no part of that which didn't sound ridiculous, but trust me, the most ridiculous part is you thinking anyone would have to coerce me into being with you."

Unable to help himself, he leaned toward her chair and captured her mouth with his. It was a transitory kiss, only meant to hold them over until later. But it ignited banked arousal in both of them. The sweet taste of her was underpinned with mutual frustration that they couldn't take this any further. Not here, anyway. He pulled away.

Part of his job tonight was to make sure couples weren't disappearing for too long into dim corners, making out a bit too fervently with their dates. What kind of example would he be setting if he dragged *his* date off to the nearest secluded corridor?

JASON'S CAR WAS SO QUIET after the sustained throbbing bass of the ballroom that Ronnie almost felt she should whisper, as if she were in church or the library. But for the first time in hours, she wasn't sure what to say. She'd already told him what a wonderful time she'd had; she'd inquired after his just-checking-in call to the Spencers to see how Emily had done this evening. The closer they got to her house, the more tongue-tied she became.

She knew what she *wanted* to ask. Was it too bold? Too soon?

Soon? She almost groaned at the irony. For the past few years, she'd lived a near-nunlike existence.

When he parked in front of her house, her heart kicked into overdrive, much like the earlier rhythmic boom from the deejay's speakers. Jason turned off the ignition and looked at her across the console, the desire in his eyes matching the rising urgency in her. She wasn't sure which one of them moved toward the other first, but they met between the seats. She threaded her fingers through the hair that brushed the nape of his neck, tilting her face up to give him better access.

This was no soft whisper of a kiss, such as they'd stolen throughout the night. This was a conflagration, a crushing kaleidoscope of emotion. At that moment, it felt like she'd wanted him forever and would do anything to have him.

Breathlessly, between the little nips he was taking at her bottom lip, she pointed out, "We'd be more comfortable inside."

He pulled away, his own breath coming in choppy pants. "All right. But don't feel like you… Kick me out whenever you want."

Her laugh was strangled. "Is that your way of saying I'm not obligated to make love with you? Because I can't think of anything I want more."

He groaned, framing her cheeks in his hands, and seized

her lips again. When they managed to break free this time, he uttered the sexiest words she'd ever heard: "Lead the way."

Ronnie's hands shook as she unlocked the front door. She'd left on a low light in the kitchen. The soft illumination spilled through the front of the house, and she chose not to reach for any of the wall switches. Instead, she faced Jason, taking advantage of the shadows to make her confession.

"I have limited experience at this," she admitted. " And it's been a *really* long time."

"For me, too. There hasn't been anyone…" His eyes widened suddenly, then he winced like a man in pain. "Ronnie, I don't have any, um, protection. I—"

"I do." The box of condoms from Lola Ann had been sort of a joke, a housewarming present Ronnie hadn't expected to use so soon.

But having the guts to use them was different in theory than practice. In the car, she'd been caught up in wanting him desperately. While she still did, she'd also had a few minutes to reflect on her lack of expertise in this area. A nervous titter escaped her.

She felt more than saw his puzzled expression. "Sorry. I seem to lack the seduction gene."

"Well, I suppose we could both promise to be very…" He trailed his index finger in a path down her neck to the hollow of her throat, where her pulse stuttered. "Gentle with each other."

Putting his words into action, he swept her hair to the side and pressed feather-light kisses against the sensitive flesh of her neck, nibbling his way up to her ear. By the time his lips again met hers, all the nerve endings in her body were tingling with heightened responsiveness. She moaned into his mouth even as she tugged at his jacket, wanting it gone so she could better feel his muscled back under her hands.

They each kicked off their shoes and made their way, hand in hand and stopping twice to kiss in her hallway, toward the bedroom. Once there, wanting to see him won out against any lingering self-consciousness. She went to the dresser to switch on a small lamp.

He walked up behind her, pulling her back as she straightened. She angled her head, expecting more of those kisses on the neck he'd been driving her pleasantly crazy with, but he surprised her by biting her earlobe. She moved restlessly against him. When she felt the hard ridge of his erection, her body burned in reaction. His right hand slid beneath the silky material of her halter top, grazing the swell of her breast, and Ronnie thought she'd melt into a puddle of need.

She wasn't sure she'd have enough muscle control to turn around, but she managed it. "I want to touch you, too," she said simply.

"Please." He unbuttoned his shirt, and her mouth went dry at the sight of his chest. Though lean, he was surprisingly well built for a literature teacher.

"You work out," she said with admiration.

He shrugged, trying to look modest but failing. "When I can. The high school has a gym."

"I'd noticed before," she admitted. "But without a shirt…"

"I like that you noticed. I like the way you look at me, Veronica."

And she liked the way he said her name—no one else had ever made it sound sexy. Tonight, she very much wanted to be sexy. She traced lazy patterns across his warm chest, then lower, over a taut abdomen and toward the top of his slacks. Cupping her face, he kissed her thoroughly.

Moving together, less gracefully than they had on the dance floor but with more purpose, they staggered toward her bed. Her thighs hit the edge of the mattress and she fell back, bringing Jason down with her, his body an intimate weight across hers. Reflexively, she raised her hips, cradling him through the fabric of her dress and panties, which were slick with arousal. He pressed against her, and her breath caught. She closed her eyes and arched involuntarily.

He unfastened the top of her dress with a manual dexterity she didn't think she could have managed under the circumstances, then dispatched the halter-style demi-cup bra with equal ease, leaving her naked from the waist up. Ronnie wasn't curvy, but he didn't look disappointed. His eyes were dark with lust, and, under his gaze, her nipples had tightened in nearly painful anticipation.

But he didn't move toward her breasts yet. Instead, he was swirling his middle finger between her collarbone and shoulder. "You have a few freckles here."

"I know." Funny, how he made them sound like an aphrodisiac.

He bent his head, kissing her in the spot he'd been touching. "And here." He moved a little to the left, repeating the action.

In an amused corner of her mind, she thought, *erotic connect-the-dots,* but then his tongue brushed over the slope of one breast and she couldn't think anymore.

When he'd suggested they be "gentle" with each other, it hadn't sounded like a form of torture, but by the time they'd shucked their remaining clothes and she'd handed him the small foil condom packet, Ronnie was nearly whimpering. He looked down at her, his smile tight with restraint but his gaze full of tenderness.

"I'm glad it's you," he said. Then he nudged against her damp, swollen flesh and slid by excruciating degrees inside her.

She was tight, and he sucked in his breath at the friction, fisting one hand in the sheet next to her and obviously fighting for self-control. His slow, exploratory foreplay had kindled such raw need that Ronnie couldn't help thrusting her hips and taking him fully. Their gazes locked. Then he began to move, withdrawing and returning until they found their rhythm. She spiraled higher and higher toward something maddeningly elusive but so sweet and fierce and magical that—

"*Oh.* Jason!"

He pumped his hips, crushing her close as he followed her over the edge. Ronnie's thoughts whirled as she tried to remember how to breathe. Oxygen didn't seem nearly as important as the man she was holding and never wanted to let go.

RONNIE TRIED TO CUDDLE peacefully in the afterglow of what they'd shared, enjoying the rise and fall of his slow, steady breathing, but she felt so invigorated.

Jason opened one eye, his laugh rumbling in his bare chest and through her body. "Why do I get the feeling you're dying to jump out of bed and go unpack boxes?"

"It's not like I don't want to be here," she said quickly.

"You're practically vibrating with energy."

"Sorry. I just feel so *good.*"

He grinned, trailing a hand over her spine. "Nice to hear."

"Can I ask you a question?"

"Ronnie, considering what just happened, you're entitled to get as personal as you want."

She propped herself up on an elbow, staring down at the face that had become so unimaginably dear to her. "If you've seen any woman socially since you came to Joyous, it's the best-kept secret in town. Women have been known to lament your seeming lack of interest in meeting anyone. I realize you were getting over a divorce and had a lot on your plate with Emily, then Sophie… I just can't help wondering, how did I get so lucky? How did we end up— Was it just because I happened to ask?" That day at the hardware store, she'd invited him to a simple lunch. Yet he'd found his way into her bed and her heart.

He smoothed a few strands of hair behind her ear. "No, it's because *you* happened to ask. I honestly didn't think I was ready to date, didn't think Emily was necessarily ready for a woman in our life. But then there was you, smiling up at me, making me laugh, making me feel things that had been dormant for so long… I'm the one who got lucky, Ronnie. It's my shocking good fortune that no other guy in this town has snapped you up long before now."

She sat up, the sheet draped low across her chest. "About that… My brothers have often felt it was their right to, um, chat with men I know. It's part of the reason I've known so few. The family's already asking questions about you. About us," she added shyly.

"For some reason, I'm reminded of Dickens." He

adopted a pseudo-spooky warning tone. "You will be visited…by Three Brothers."

Chuckling, she shoved at his shoulder. "The good news is that Will lives in North Carolina, so it will probably only be two." Of course, Will was coming for Easter.

"Ronnie, I'd like to meet your family."

"You only say that because you don't really know them. Run, save yourself."

"They're a big part of your life. I want to know the people who are important to you, just like I hope you and Em will get to know each other better."

There was that twinge again, in the pit of her stomach. Not that she didn't want to get to know his daughter, but this was moving so fast….

He sat up next to her, still smiling, but she could see the traces of uncertainty in his eyes. "You're not ashamed of me, are you?" he kidded.

"Of course not! You're wonderful." That earned her a kiss.

Which led to another. And another, until they eventually found a good use for all that restive energy Ronnie had been experiencing.

Chapter Eight

The earliest streaks of dawn were stealing through the bedroom window, accompanied by twitters of birdsong outside. Though Ronnie knew Jason had to leave, it was so tempting to ask him to stay just a bit longer. She was glad her little house was slightly off the beaten path and not in a subdivision, where the car in her driveway throughout the night might have invited comment.

Even after looking her fill last night at his body, she watched unabashedly as he dressed. The hours of intimate exploration hadn't been limited only to sex, but to small discoveries…his appendectomy scar, the small birthmark on his shoulder blade. For his part, Jason had had entirely too much fun cataloging every freckle he could find scattered across her body.

Just the memory stirred warm longing in her. *Don't go.*

But he wasn't free to laze in her bed half the morning. He'd told her that his daughter was an early riser and there was no telling how soon the Spencers would bring her home. Jason needed time to get back and clean up, possibly chug a pot of coffee to revive him after the sleepless night.

"You shouldn't get up, though," he told her, pressing a

quick kiss to her forehead. "Stay in bed, get some rest. Dream of me?"

She would. Probably not now, because she doubted she'd be able to sleep after listening to him drive away, but over time, she was sure his kisses would haunt her dreams and fantasies. No man had ever touched her like that before. Ronnie's limited sexual encounters had been mostly brief, with well-meaning guys who'd possessed more gusto than finesse.

"I'll call you soon," he said, giving her one last kiss goodbye.

He walked himself out, and she ran her tongue across her lips, as if sealing the imprint of him there. Then she rolled on her side and nuzzled the pillow he'd used, breathing in the faint remainder of his scent. Knowing her mind wasn't nearly calm enough for sleep, she kicked the covers aside and decided she might as well start her day. Heaven knew she had plenty to do around the house to keep her busy.

She jumped into the shower, trying to get her thoughts organized, but the hot, pulsing spray against her sensitized skin and agreeably aching muscles conjured steamy scenes from the previous hours. She indulged herself in replaying her favorite memories from the night. Not just here, but earlier, when her knees had trembled at their first kiss, or when he'd made her laugh on the dance floor. It took the water turning increasingly cold for her to realize she was standing there grinning like an idiot. She blinked, coming back to her senses and twisting the faucet.

Reaching for her towel, she froze suddenly as a sound cut through the stillness of the house. Tilting her head, she listened carefully. Was her phone ringing? Not many people would call her this early in the morning, especially on the weekend. Could it be Jason? A half smile played about her mouth. He *did* say he'd call soon.

With the towel wrapped around her and her bangs dripping droplets of water in her eyes, she hurried to the phone on her nightstand. "Hello?"

"Ronnie?" It was Lola Ann. "I probably woke you up, I'm sorry. I was just really hoping that maybe you were free for breakfast."

"Actually, I was awake."

"Then how about I bring over some food? I could use someone to talk to."

"Ditto."

BY A QUARTER TILL EIGHT, Lola Ann had arrived with a dozen doughnuts from the Bestest Bakery.

Ronnie, wearing an old flannel shirt of Danny's over a pair of plaid pajama bottoms, smiled at the selection. Chocolate-frosted cake doughnuts, glazed doughnuts with chocolate filling, devil's food with chocolate sprinkles... "I sense a theme," she said, filling two glasses with milk.

Sighing, Lola Ann sat in one of the mismatched dinette chairs Ronnie planned to strip and paint. Each chair would eventually be a different primary color with white cushions and set around a white tabletop.

"Last night, I inadvertently ate half a container of chocolate frosting," Lola Ann admitted. "When a girl's got romantic troubles, *why* can't she crave broccoli and green tea to make her feel better?"

Romantic troubles? Ronnie waded in gently. "So, should I assume this in some way involves my brother?"

Lola Ann winced. "I'm a terrible friend. I should be

asking how your big date went, not whining about my own problems."

"She who brings the doughnuts gets the floor first What's up?"

"I had a date last night." Lola Ann looked about as excited as someone who just learned their car needs thousands of dollars of repair.

"With who?"

"Bear. He came by the library to drop off a book for his aunt, except that I think it might have been an excuse to see me."

Ronnie almost smiled—the librarian-wooing equivalent of phantom engine noises.

"It was almost closing time when he came by, and there was no one else there. He asked where I was headed after work, if I maybe wanted to grab dinner with him or go bowling. We did both.

"And it was fun," Lola Ann said miserably. "The same kind of platonic, no-sparks fun I might have with you if you were about a foot taller. He kissed me at the end of the date."

Ronnie wrinkled her nose. "No good?"

"I don't know. I was too busy wondering how it would compare to one of Devin's kisses. This has gone past the point of ridiculousness." Lola Ann took a big chomp out of one of the chocolate-glazed doughnuts.

Once she'd swallowed, she explained, "I've known your brother for a long time, and these feelings have been escalating. But it was easier not to do anything about it when you didn't have a guy in your life, either. You know what I mean? I don't want to sound like I'm just jealous you've found someone to spend Saturday nights with. It's more that you've galvanized me. I can't help but wonder what would have happened if I'd asked your brother to lunch one day."

"I don't know, but you still can."

"I'm going to have to. When Bear left last night, he smiled and said he'd see me around. I don't think he'll ask me out again. It's not like he appeared heartbroken, but he's a good guy. Cute, in his way. Sweet, steady. Shouldn't I date *him* instead of pining after your stupid brother? No offense."

Ronnie laughed. "None taken."

"I think I have to try to get Devin's attention, let him know how I feel, for better or worse. If it leads to disaster—which I think we both know is probable—then at least I know I tried and can move on. Be emotionally available for the next sweet, steady guy who comes along." She took another bite of doughnut, then smiled. "Give me some incentive, tell me things are going well between you and Jason. Did you have a good time last night? I was hoping you'd call when you got in so I could hear all about it, but it was probably late."

"Actually, it was pretty early...when he left this morning."

"Veronica! You guys...?"

"Oh, yes." Three times, each seemingly better than the one before because she felt closer and closer to him.

"Wow." Lola Ann shook her head, then said it again. "Wow. So I guess things are serious?"

Ronnie swiped a bit of frosting off the top of her doughnut. "They feel serious." Never before had the idiom *falling for someone* seemed so appropriate; it was as if she teetered on a precipice.

Lola Ann frowned. "You don't sound as happy as I would have imagined."

"No, I...I realize everybody has their own baggage they

bring to a relationship, but he has a daughter. An adorable one, absolutely, but kids were not on my radar. Not anytime soon." She glanced around the small, out-of-date kitchen, recalling her fierce joy when she'd first calculated that she could afford this place. She'd been looking forward to the independent solitude, the not needing to cook for anyone else, to the waking up in the morning wondering *what next* instead of feeling as if it had already been thrust upon her. "After Mom died, I remember feeling responsible for Dad and the boys even though I was the youngest. I'm just not sure I'm ready to be responsible for anyone else right now."

"Have you told Jason that?" Lola Ann asked gently.

"Before last night, it felt premature to *think,* much less say, 'Jason, even though we've only been on like a date and a half, in case you were planning to propose marriage, you should know I have mixed feelings on being a stepmother.'"

Granted, after their marathon lovemaking and his statement that he wanted her to become closer to Emily, it seemed like a more relevant conversation now.

"Men." Lola Ann let out an exaggerated sigh. "They sure complicate life. Think they're worth all the trouble they cause?"

Only one way to find out.

WHEN RONNIE WALKED INTO the office on the Monday following her date with Jason, three pairs of eyes fixed expectantly on her. After her last insistence that she was a grown-up capable of making her own romantic decisions, her father and brothers had stopped interrogating her outright. But their curiosity and concern were palpable.

A peal of laughter escaped her. "Y'all are just sad." A

trio of six-foot mother hens. *Well, of course they are.* Like her, they'd tried in their own imperfect ways to fill the void.

"We love you," Wayne said gruffly.

"I love you, too. But what are we all doing in here when there are repairs that need to be made?"

"Hey, don't look at me," Danny said. "I'm an office drone, I'm supposed to be here. By the way, Ronnie, I signed for an early-morning delivery of that fuel pump you ordered."

"Great, I'll bet Mr. Jacobs is looking forward to getting his truck back." She passed by her brothers, toward the bays, stopping when she realized that her father was studying her. "Wh-what?"

He shook his head. "I don't know. You just…"

Averting her gaze, she was transported back to that morning years ago after she'd lost her virginity, when she'd been convinced her father would be able to tell somehow just by looking at her.

"I guess that new house agrees with you," he told her fondly, preceding her through the door.

Devin smirked, addressing her in a low tone. "The house. Yeah, that must be it."

She rolled her eyes at her brother's double standard. With him—the guy who dated freely and frequently—she experienced none of the quasi guilt she'd felt in front of Wayne. Dev was hardly the poster child for celibacy and had no right to want her to be.

"We'll really miss you when construction work picks back up," she said with patented, little-sister fake sweetness. A torrent of spring rain yesterday and forecasted thunderstorms throughout this week had postponed the job he'd been scheduled to start today.

As she zipped up her coveralls, she couldn't help wondering if Devin was truly happy behind his teasing smiles. He certainly seemed to be, with the carefree bachelor's life she'd often envied through the kitchen window, but maybe that was a facade. The most incredible part of her date with Jason had been how connected she'd felt to him, and somehow, she doubted Devin had experienced any real connection with a woman in a long time. Mentally, she crossed her fingers that, if and when Lola Ann got up the nerve to tell Devin about her feelings, he was smart enough to realize it might be the opportunity for something special.

Then, putting her brother's love life behind her, she got to work.

However, throughout the day, her own love life crept up on her in unexpected ways. In one of the quieter lulls, she caught part of a melody from her dad's radio and realized it was a song she and Jason had danced to. Lost in the memory of being in his arms, smiling into his eyes, she almost over-tightened a cam belt. While Devin and her father talked about basketball, she found herself wondering if Jason followed sports, too. It would give him something innocuous to discuss with her brothers when he formally came over to meet them, which seemed inevitable. Besides, Ronnie was a big football fan herself—she had a tantalizing image of curling up on her couch with Jason for a weekend Titans game, making out during halftime. Autumn was months away. Would they be together? Entertaining pleasant what-ifs, she considered a behind-closed-doors Halloween costume for Jason's eyes only; having a date seated next to her for the first time at the family Thanksgiving table; going shopping with Lola Ann or Charity to pick out his Christmas present.

With a start, she realized that while her various day-dreams had a lot of common themes, they also had one missing element in common: Emily.

Christmas for Jason would not be strategically hung mistletoe, breakfast in bed and a quiet exchange of romantic gifts. There would be staying up late, or getting up early, to play Santa, little fingers sticky with candy canes, maybe grandparents. Would his family come visit? Would he even be in town? Maybe he'd take Emily to see her relatives for the holidays. Come to think of it, did he ever talk to her relatives on *Isobel's* side of the family? Here she was thinking in terms of abstract romantic tableaus, but the reality—

Splash. The mild burning and stringent fumes were a none-too-subtle reminder that she'd forgotten to siphon out the gas before starting. She cursed, using a particularly foul phrase that had been a favorite of Danny's during his college years.

"You all right?" Wayne asked her as she cleaned herself up at the industrial sink.

"Yeah." She hadn't made stupid rookie mistakes like that even when she *was* a rookie. "I'm gonna stink and probably people shouldn't smoke within ten feet of me, but it didn't hit me anywhere critical." And, very fortunately for her, the vehicle's owner had let the tank get down to practically empty.

Her dad didn't lecture her over the basics of doing her job, but he did volunteer her half an hour later to go pick up a late lunch for everyone. With a sigh, she took everyone's orders and promised to swing by the bank and make a deposit for Danny.

Twenty minutes later, she stood inside Adam's Ribs
The long line, despite the noon hour having already passed
attested to the place's popularity. When someone in the
crowded interior jostled her, Ronnie turned to automatically
accept an apology. She found herself looking at a uniformed
police officer with a familiar face, but she drew a blank on
his name. His partner, Harvey Mars, however, had been in
her graduating class. Both men held half-eaten sandwiches

"Hey, Harvey. How's it going?"

"Just got a 911," he told her. He eyed her Carter & Sons
cap. "You have the truck here?"

"The tow truck?" She shook her head. "I'm in my car."

"Accident over on Main," Harvey's partner explained.

She fell into step with them, figuring she could come
back for food when the line had died down. "Why don't
follow you over and see if the truck's needed? Do you
know how serious it was?"

"Two cars," Harvey said. "Person who called it in said
a woman ran a red light and is banged up. Possible
broken bones."

The drive across to Main only took a minute. As she ap
proached, Ronnie could see a dented pickup off to the side
of the road, with a compact car still sitting at a diagonal in
the middle of the intersection. She flipped her blinker on
and started to turn left; the sun glinted off an object in the
road, catching her eye. Probably a piece of glass or metal
from… No. In a flash of almost dizzying recognition, she
realized she was looking at a tiara on the asphalt.

Her gaze darted back to the shoulder. This time she
took closer inventory of the people at the scene—includ
ing an EMT carrying a dark-haired little girl into an am

bulance. Ronnie's heart pounded, sending dread and adrenaline through her body. Her instinct was to floor her own car and reach her destination that much sooner, but reason prevailed. The last thing she needed to do was cause another accident.

Still, once she'd parked, she hopped out of her car and sprinted toward the medical team. "Emily? Are you all right? Is she all right?" She grabbed the arm of another EMT, a tall black man with kind eyes.

"The little girl?" He nodded, his voice gravelly but reassuring. "She's okay, just shaken. We're taking her babysitter in for X-rays. The girl's father should be here any second."

They'd called Jason at school, no doubt. God, he must be terrified. Even if she'd been told her child was all right, Ronnie would be scared to death until she'd confirmed it with her own eyes.

"Can I wait with her until her dad gets here? I'm a friend of the family."

The man nodded again. "That would be great, then we can go ahead and take the woman on to the hospital."

Emily sat in the back of the ambulance, wide-eyed and silent as a tearful woman tried to reassure her. "I'm okay, baby. I'm just so sorry."

Nina Bruner. Ronnie placed the woman as someone who'd been in the garage this summer for an estimate on a new air conditioner she'd ultimately decided she couldn't afford.

"Hi, Nina." Ronnie gave her a sympathetic smile. "I hear you hurt your arm. Have they already given you something for the pain?"

The woman's sobbing increased. "Ronnie! Oh, I should have brought the car in. The brakes were squeaky, but with the rain…I thought they were wet. I tried to stop for the light, but we just slid into that poor man."

"He's just fine," an EMT told Nina soothingly.

"Yes, but his car. My car. And Emily! If she'd been hurt…" The woman shot another distraught gaze to the pale-faced girl.

"Nina, calm down. You don't want to scare Emily." Ronnie took the little girl's hand. "They need to take you in and get a cast on that arm and check for other injuries. I'll stay until Jason gets here, okay?"

"Tell him I'm sorry. I'm so sorry."

As the EMTs closed the ambulance doors, Ronnie squatted down on the grass, at Emily's eye level. "Hey, there. You remember me, right?"

"Ronnie." But she had trouble with her *R*s and it came out Wonnie. "We had ice cream. After the princess movie. My princess crown fell out the window." Her bottom lip trembled.

Ronnie scooped the girl up in her arms and pointed Harvey toward the tiara. It hadn't snapped completely in half, but it was definitely fractured. Tears rolled down the girl's smooth cheeks, each one a little stab in Ronnie's heart.

"I know it's not as cool as a princess crown, but I have a special hat in my car. Like mine." Ronnie pointed toward the Carter & Sons denim cap she wore, her ponytail threaded through the adjustable strap in back. "Would you like it?"

Emily thought this over, then nodded. She was sniffling as they walked to Ronnie's parked car, but there weren't any more tears.

Ronnie popped open her glove compartment and retrieved the folded cap. She sat cross-legged on the ground next to the little girl. "Here, let's see how this looks." Even

t the smallest size-setting, it fell low over Emily's
orehead, causing her to tilt her head back at an exagger-
ted angle to see.

"I keep it?" the girl asked shyly.

"You bet. It's—"

"Emily!" Jason's shout was a combination of terror and
elief as he barreled toward them.

With the intention of meeting him halfway, Ronnie
icked Emily up, settling the little girl on her hip, but
Ronnie hadn't taken two steps before Jason reached them.
Ie squashed both females into a tight hug that had Emily
queaking.

"Daddy!"

"Sorry, sweet pea." He loosened his grip slightly but
idn't let go. "Where's Nina? Is she all right?"

Ronnie craned her head around the child they held
ogether. "I think her arm's broken. The EMTs took her. It
ooks like the accident was caused by brake failure. She's
laming herself, wanted me to tell you how sorry she is."

"Emily and I will take her some flowers at the hospital.
Ronnie, thank you for—" His cell phone buzzed, and he
lanced at the view screen. "Nina's husband. Will you stay
vith Emily while I take this?"

"Sure." He probably wanted to ask about Nina's condi-
on without further alarming Emily. Ronnie smiled at the
ttle girl. "So…do you know your ABCs?"

The alphabet proved to be too taxing for such a stress-
ul afternoon, but they were on their second round of
Twinkle, Twinkle Little Star" when Jason returned to say
at Nina had broken her arm and her collarbone.

"You tell her that I'm working on a get-well present,"

Ronnie said, "and that her brakes will be working like new when she's ready to drive again. No charge for the labor.

Jason leaned down to kiss her hard and fast on the lips

Twin currents of shock and sensation ran through her Though he'd kissed her countless times on Saturday, tha hadn't been on the public streets of town. In front of hi kid. Before she could figure out how to respond, he' jerked back, the apology clear in his eyes.

"I should probably apologize for that," he said sounding bemused.

"Well…emotions are running high." Her own ha been rioting uncontrollably since she'd arrived on scene she couldn't begin to imagine how *he* felt, what it woul be like to get that call at work that your child had bee in an accident.

"Daddy, are you putting Ronnie to bed?"

"What?" Did the fact that Ronnie had unintentionall shrieked at a not-quite-three-year-old who'd just been in car accident mean she'd be an unfit parent?

"Daddy kisses me night-night. And at naptime." Emil wrinkled her nose at this, emphasizing her dislike for nap:

Jason cleared his throat. "When people care abou each other, they hug and kiss sometimes. Like you, lik Gran. I care about Ronnie. A lot," he added, meeting he eyes briefly.

After thinking this over for a second, Emily demon strated her own affection by throwing her little body int an unexpected hug around Ronnie's knees, threatening t unbalance her. "I care, too! But your perfume is stinky."

Ronnie pulled away, forcing a laugh. "Oh, that's…

uh, had a small mishap with some gasoline this morning."
Prompting her father to send her out so she could clear her head.

Ironic, since now she had more to think about than ever.

Chapter Nine

Except for sounds of the old house settling and the refrigerator running, the house was quiet as Jason graded essays. Or tried to grade, anyway; he'd promised the students updates on their semester averages. But his mind kept flashing back to that horrific phone call earlier. Because of thunder last night, Emily hadn't been able to sleep; in the wake of the call telling him "there's been an accident," Jason felt as if he might never sleep peacefully again. There'd be too many images and possible outcomes awaiting him.

The caller had prefaced their commentary with "Mr. McDeere, there's absolutely no need to panic." Which, ironically, had paralyzed him with fear. It was a miracle he'd been able to get out the words "What's happened to Emily?"

Bumps and bruises, nothing a pink adhesive bandage couldn't fix, they'd promised him. Yet his heartbeat hadn't slowed to normal until he'd been able to get to her himself. The picture of Ronnie and his daughter rose in his mind like a stirring, symphonic swell of music, so piercingly sweet that he ached with it. If he'd thought he was affected that night at the ice cream parlor, seeing their heads close and hearing them laugh together, it was nothing compared to today—his small child cradled protectively by the woman he might be falling in love with, both of them wearing matching caps as Ronnie gently soothed away the last of Em's tears.

Oh, yes. He could definitely fall for her. Letting out a sigh, he realized his body had tensed when he recalled the accident and the potential danger to his daughter and that thoughts of Ronnie had centered him. His shoulders rolled back to their normal posture instead of at rigid attention. Without even being present, Ronnie had comforted him just as she'd comforted his little girl.

Everything is going to be all right.

Except that a few of his honors students, paying close attention to the GPA race to valedictorian, were going to come after him with sharp objects if he didn't get this grading done. He returned to the essays, some of the observations making him wince, others making him chuckle. He'd barely started an opening paragraph about Mark Twain's writing when a shriek split the peace.

Jason bolted out of the small chair so quickly it almost toppled. He hurried to his daughter's room and found her sitting up in bed, sobbing.

"It's okay, I'm here." He gathered her against his chest, smoothing her hair. "Shh. Did you have a bad dream?" It was raining again, but without all the dramatic flashes of lightning and booming thunder that had scared her the night before.

She nodded, her entire body shivering. She wasn't small for her age, but tonight she felt more fragile than porcelain.

"Do you remember what it was about?" he asked gently.

Sometimes, when it was an imaginary terror like a monster under the bed, he could make up silly stories about the monster that made her laugh.

Her only answer was a hiccup, followed by the fidgeting that he'd learned meant she needed to use the bathroom. He helped her in, then tucked her back in bed, staying by her side until her breathing had become even and deep. But hours later, after he'd gone to bed himself, he opened his eyes to find his daughter standing by his bed, leaning so close that it was almost startling.

"Emily?"

She was crying, dragging her comforter behind her. "I had a bad dream about the car. I want Ronnie."

The declaration left him poleaxed. Though Emily had mentioned Ronnie at the park over spring break, mostly in the hopes of having a new playmate, it was always *him* his daughter wanted when she was upset. She'd never even specifically requested her mother, Isobel having left during Em's infancy. After Gran died, his daughter had asked for her once or twice, but that was all. Maybe her reaction now was due to Ronnie being the first person who'd arrived to help her today.

"It's really, really late, sweet pea. Ronnie's asleep at her house."

Emily's crying worsened, not the howls of a toddler tantrum, but small broken whimpers that shredded his soul.

He shoved a hand through his hair, half tempted to dial Ronnie's number if it would bring his daughter peace. Instead, he flipped back the half of the comforter next to him. "Do you want to sleep in here?"

She nodded.

That's what they'd wound up doing the night before, too, when she was frightened. Was he creating bad habits, setting patterns that would be hard to break? There was a time for tough parenting, but surely this wasn't it. She was his baby; he couldn't consign her to facing her fears alone.

Meanwhile, he was wondering if he knew what the hell he was doing. Every day, there were a hundred little pitfalls, mistakes he might be making and would only recognize in hindsight. Parenting was more like an essay test than multiple choice; sometimes there were no clear-cut answers.

For days after Isobel's departure, he'd been convinced his wife was coming back—she would miss her husband and child, she would see her doctor and try new medicines to help her cope. When he'd realized that wasn't the case, he'd adopted a grimly determined "you and me, kid" attitude, telling himself he and Emily didn't need anyone but each other. Of course, after several months of that egotistical nonsense, he'd retreated here for Gran's help. She'd been a wise, patient woman, and he missed her. But the pangs he'd been feeling lately weren't just mourning. For the first time since his marriage dissolved, what he wanted was an equal partner, someone to worry with him when Em was running high fevers, laugh with him when she used the wrong word with comical results, someone to be a sounding board and let him know if he was screwing up.

Who was he kidding? He didn't want a faceless, nameless "someone."

He helped Emily onto the mattress, plumping the extra pillow for her. "You don't have to be scared. Miss Nina's going to be okay, and Ronnie's fixing her car so that it shouldn't have any more accidents, all right?"

"Can Ronnie come play with me tomorrow?"

"No, she has to do her job during the day, just like Daddy."

Emily yawned, then repeated stubbornly, "Want Ronnie."

He couldn't blame her. *So do I.*

ACTING ON IMPULSE, RONNIE strolled into the high school where she and all three of her brothers had attended years earlier. The hall wasn't mobbed, but there were a few students lingering, probably on their way to the cafeteria for lunch. Carrying her pink gift bag, she felt silly and conspicuous and made a note to avoid acting on impulse from now on.

But if you hadn't been spontaneous, you might never have gotten to know Jason this way. Whatever else happened and however nervous she might be about him being a single father, she would never take back the last couple of weeks and all that had passed between them.

She'd left her customary cap in the car, finger-combed her hair and applied fresh lip gloss. It was as presentable as she was going to get for the middle of a Tuesday that was so uncharacteristically humid that she felt like she needed gills to breathe. As she walked down the main corridor to the office, where all visitors were required to check in, she noticed a couple of teenage boys watching her.

One of them nudged his friend, eyeing Ronnie's beribboned bag and calling, "So, are you, like, the birthday-gram girl?"

Drawing on experience dealing with irritating brothers, she raised her eyebrows and blasted him with a look that sent him scurrying off to wherever he was supposed to be. Moments later, she was pushing open the glass door to the administrative office.

The receptionist took in the present and smiled. "Are you here to have a birthday lunch with your…"

Say kid and I'll cry. Ronnie would hate to think she looked old enough to have a teenager.

"Um, younger sister?" the woman guessed.

Ronnie grinned. "Actually, I was hoping to meet with one of your teachers, if that's permissible. I believe he has a free period right now."

"Veronica, is that you?"

She turned to find Principal Schonrock smiling quizzically. "Yes, ma'am. I was hoping I could borrow Jason for a minute. Um, Mr. McDeere." The teacher title seemed more appropriate inside the building.

The principal laughed. "I saw the two of you dancing at Spring Fling, so I'm pretty sure you're allowed to be on a first-name basis. Step out into the hall with me and I'll point the way to his classroom. I believe he's in there." She glanced down to the sparkly pink bag but didn't say anything.

"It's for his daughter," Ronnie said. "That's why I'm here, to drop it off."

"Yes, I know he was very worried about her when he tore out of here yesterday. Nice seeing you again, Veronica. And I'm sure Jason will be delighted." She returned to the office, whistling softly.

Ronnie followed the principal's directions to Jason's class, and her heart gave an absurd little leap when she saw him sitting behind his desk, books and papers sprawled across the surface, a homework assignment written on the chalkboard behind him. She envied the kids he taught; she'd love to sit here for an hour, watching while he carried on an animated conversation about characters and stories he loved.

As if he could feel her gaze on him, he jerked his head up, his expression transforming into a bright smile once he saw her. "Ronnie! Come in, come in. What are you doing here?"

"I have something for the munchkin." She walked to the front of the room, setting the gift on his desk—although she was hard-pressed to find a spot for it amid the clutter. "I thought I'd drop this off and maybe get an update on Nina."

"They kept her overnight for observation because she had a concussion in addition to the broken right arm and bruised ribs. She was overjoyed when I told her about the car and the bargain repairs you were doing, she and her husband have had a tough year financially. I promised her I wouldn't hire anyone permanent to replace her, that the job's hers again as soon as she can manage. Wanda Spencer's pinch-hitting for me today." He ran a hand through his hair—obviously not the first time he'd done so. It was beginning to stand on end.

"Why don't I call my sister-in-law for you?" she volunteered. "Kaitlyn might know some babysitters. Or even be able to help you out a few days herself."

"You're a lifesaver. There's a teenager I trust enough to use for a few hours on the weekend, but she's not available during school hours." He darted a quick glance to check the empty doorway, then leaned across the desk to give her a kiss so brief it was more tease than caress. "Thank you."

"For offering to call Kaitlyn?"

"For *everything*," he said firmly. He jabbed an index finger toward the gift bag. "May I peek?"

"Of course." She shifted her weight, rocking on the balls of her feet. "It's really nothing. I just…" She hadn't been able to get Emily's wide eyes, huge in that pale face, out of her mind.

Jason gingerly pried the edges of the bag apart to get a look at the contents: a glittery crown, matching scepter and a purple-and-silver feather boa. Then he favored her with a gaze so warm that she almost fanned herself. "You're amazing."

Her urge to fidget grew. "It was just a quick stop at the dollar store."

"It will be invaluable to Em. I don't know if you'll believe this, based on how she acts around you, but it normally takes her a while to open up around someone. She really likes you. A testament to her good people instincts," he said proudly. "As it happens, I have something she wanted me to give you."

She blinked. "You do?"

Sliding open the top drawer of his desk, he nodded. "She colored it this morning, and I was planning to stop by the garage later to give it to you. Here."

He handed her a piece of spiral notebook paper that had been folded in half and marked up with considerable amounts of pink and purple crayon, mostly in jagged lines and loops.

"Ah." She studied the artwork, wondering if it was abstract or if there were supposed to be actual objects rendered in the drawing. Her dad liked to tell the story about a clay animal Ronnie had once made for Mother's Day. She barely remembered it. Apparently, she'd insisted the figurine was a panda bear, while her brothers all thought it looked like a dinosaur and her father had hesitantly guessed a giraffe. Sue Carter had taken one look at it, somehow known immediately it was a panda bear (possibly a lucky guess because that had been Ronnie's favorite animal at the time) and pronounced it perfect. Clearly, Ronnie didn't have that intuitive talent.

Jason helped her out. "It's an invitation. To her birthday party. She turns three the Saturday after Easter. We're having a little get-together in the backyard. I'll cook out. We *both* hope you can come."

She glanced again at the piece of paper, but this time the harmless lines seemed like coiled rope, tangles that might trip her up if she took a wrong step.

"Ronnie? Everything okay?"

Honestly, she didn't know. "You said yourself that Emily likes me," she began slowly.

"Yeah. That's a good thing. Right?"

"She saw us kissing yesterday, and you gave her a good explanation. But what will you tell her if the circumstances…?" She didn't like to think about them not being together, but wasn't it too soon to assume that they would stay this way? "How will it affect her if you and I keep dating and it doesn't work out between us?"

"Ronnie, I think you and I are wonderful together, and I see no reason not to pursue that." He reached out to brush his knuckles over her cheek. "It's a shame that there aren't any guarantees that I can give you, or Em, but even being married to her mother wasn't a guarantee that she'd be with us a year down the road."

Thinking about her own mother, Ronnie had to acknowledge that he was right: there were no guarantees. Somehow, that didn't make her feel any better.

"I try not to think in negative terms about the what-ifs. Not that I'm always successful," he admitted, the corner of his mouth curling up in a slightly self-deprecating smile. "And of course I want to be…cautious, for my daughter's sake. I want to be open to happiness, though, too. For both our sakes."

On the one hand, she was flattered and buoyed by his words. *You and I are wonderful together.* But the nerves in her stomach persisted. "You really see me, down the road, as potential wife and mommy material?" She wished she could see herself that way.

Wouldn't Emily be better off with a more put-together, worldly woman who knew how to bake birthday cakes and would eventually teach her daughter how to accessorize with something other than a denim cap? Ronnie still squabbled with her brothers and watched cartoons. She'd dated much too seldom to give sound dating advice and couldn't name a single designer of clothes, purses or shoes. *Now, hers on the other hand...*

"Ronnie, when I look at you, I see—" The clanging bell overhead cut off his words.

"I'm guessing that means the next period will start soon and students will trickle in any moment now?"

"Yeah, but—"

"I should be going." *Coward.* Yet acknowledging that she was taking the spineless way out didn't stem her instinct to flee.

She and Jason had a problem. It wasn't one she'd wanted to acknowledge before now, because it made her feel petty. What was wrong with her? A woman with more sense would spend her spare moments doodling *Mrs. Jason McDeere* on the garage letterhead. Hundreds of men in the world like her brother, who avoided real intimacy, and Ronnie had been lucky enough to meet a man who wanted to consider all the possibilities...even the permanent ones! Shouldn't she be hoping that they fell madly in love and that she could be Emily's substitute mommy?

After all, who knew better than Ronnie what it was li[ke] to reach milestones and yearn for a mother to share the[m] with? To come home after a bad day at school and want mom there to help with homework and offer you fres[h] from-the-oven cookies? *Yeah, except, your cookies ha[ve] the consistency of hockey pucks, and unless she neede[d] help with shop homework, she'd be better off looking to h[er] better-educated father.* Ronnie and Devin had only do[ne] regional vocational school, not the full four years of colleg[e] Danny and Will had accomplished.

Yet each time she'd experienced these misgivings, she'[d] rationalized that it was too soon to worry about this. Sh[e] didn't want to give up this newfound relationship. Now, sh[e] asked herself with a sigh, when exactly *was* the appropri[?] ate time to panic over the thought of becoming an insta[nt] mommy—months from now, when Emily had grown eve[n] more attached and started asking if she could be the flowe[r] girl in the wedding?

"TURNABOUT'S FAIR PLAY, RIGHT? Me coming to see you [at] your work?"

The voice behind her caused Ronnie to jump, spillin[g] coffee grinds over her hand. She'd come in early to finis[h] up work on Nina Bruner's car when she was on her ow[n] time instead of on the clock. The garage wasn't technical[ly] open yet, but she hadn't bothered to lock the door behin[d] her. Wayne Carter would be arriving in the next fe[w] minutes, and she'd planned to have coffee brewed f[or] both of them.

She slanted a reproachful look over her shoulder as s[he] finished scooping dark roast into the filter. "You scared me[.]

"Sorry." Jason ducked his head. "I figured you heard me come in."

It was embarrassing to admit how preoccupied she'd been this week—and that he was the cause of it. "I'm a little out of it. Didn't sleep well last night," she admitted. Hence the immediate and pressing need for more caffeine before she started working on anyone's automobile.

"There's a lot of that going around," Jason said as he approached. "The not sleeping, I mean."

She studied him. His face was shadowed with uncharacteristic stubble and circles, which should have made his eyes less gorgeous, but didn't. Her heart constricted with concern. "You look awful."

"Emily hasn't slept through the night since this weekend. It feels like I get two consecutive hours tops, then it takes me a long time to fall back asleep because I'm worrying about her."

"Poor kid. And poor you."

He barely seemed to hear her. "She wakes up crying, and she...well, she's asked for you more than once."

"Me?"

Even Ashley, who adored Aunt Ronnie, wanted her mother or father when she was scared or hurt. It struck her as unbearably sad that Emily would cling to a woman she'd only seen on two separate occasions.

Jason shrugged. "You made an impression."

Or the kid's desperate, trying to create family members like her friends have. Emily's mother had abandoned her, one grandmother lived out West, the other had passed away, and because Jason and Isobel were both only children, Em didn't even have a cool aunt. Frankly, it was a lot of pressure for any female role model who happened into the girl's life, the voids that needed to be filled.

They stared at each other, neither saying anything, nor retracing steps to the potential land-mine conversation they'd begun in his classroom yesterday. But it was clearly between them.

"If you stay another minute or two, I can pour you a cup of coffee," she said. Though part of her suspected she wouldn't feel balanced again until he left, the rest of her wanted to give him excuses to hang around awhile. "By the way, I did phone Kaitlyn last night. She's going to call you this evening about possible babysitting."

"Thank you. I don't know what I'd do without you." He gave her a weary smile. "Actually, I do. I know what it's like to do this completely on my own. It *sucks*. It's nice to have someone else pitch in."

The fact that he sounded so genuinely grateful created the same pang in her chest as the news that Ronnie had made Emily's top-ten list of people to cry for in the night. In a perfect world, Emily would be so surrounded by adults who loved and cared for her that a woman who'd once taken her to use the restroom at an ice cream emporium wouldn't even register as a blip on the radar.

This time when the office door opened, Ronnie did notice—she and Jason both turned to find her father, with a copy of the *Joyous Journal-Report* folded under one arm and a mildly surprised expression on his face.

He addressed her first. "Morning, Ronnie."

"Hey, Daddy. I don't know if the two of you have formally met in town, but this is Jason McDeere. Jason, my father, Wayne Carter."

The two men shook hands. "Nice to meet you, Mr. Carter."

Wayne looked him square in the eye. "I've heard lots of
ood things about you. All the same, I would take it amiss
' anyone hurt Ronnie."

"So would I, sir," Jason said over top of her groaned
rotest.

"Good answer." Wayne shot Ronnie a glance of such
latant approval that he might as well have accompanied
 with a thumbs-up sign. "I didn't mean to interrupt
 hatever you two kids were discussing. Is it going to
other anyone if I read the paper at one of the desks here?"
 here weren't any chairs out in the repair bays.

"Not at all. I just dropped in to ask Ronnie a question,
 en I need to get to work myself." Jason turned to her. "I
 ld you Em's been having nightmares. She also gets wide-
 yed whenever I put her in the car. I know you're busy and
 at the garage probably isn't a safe place for kids to be
 nderfoot, but could I bring her by some time? I thought
 e could show her that you're fixing Miss Nina's car.
 laybe if you could tell her something basic about how cars
 ork, Emily will feel less afraid. Sound stupid?"

Ronnie shook her head. "Sometimes the unknown is
 :arier just because it is unknown, right?" She had no idea
 his plan would work, but she was willing to try.

"Exactly. You could demystify the monster for her."

She craned her head to see her father on the other side
 f Jason. To give Wayne credit for respecting her privacy,
 : was trying really hard to look like he wasn't listening.
)ad, you okay with me giving Emily a guided tour later
 the week?"

"As long as she understands the tools aren't toys, it

should be fine. You and your brothers weren't much olde
when I first started bringing you in."

She'd grown up here as much as she had in the house
She recalled one afternoon when her mom was exhauste
in the early days of her treatment and wanted a quiet fev
hours to herself so she could sleep. The boys had all beer
older, off involved in different clubs and intramural spor
practices. But Wayne had brought Ronnie to the garage an
taught her how to change a tire while rain fell softly outsid
the raised bay door. Glancing around, she wondered if th
gritty, cavernous space had something to offer a little gir
who liked pink princesses and sparkly tiaras. Thinkin
back to how her dad had put her at ease that long-ago af
ternoon, how he'd made her feel special and safe, Ronni
knew it was worth a shot.

"Saturday morning?" she suggested.

"Thank you." Jason looked as if he wanted to kiss he
They both slid surreptitious glances toward Wayne an
exchanged lukewarm platonic goodbyes.

After Jason left, her father commented, "I like him."

"He's a good guy." She tried to keep her tone casua
Under different circumstances, she would have been happ
about her dad's endorsement. At the moment, it just adde
to an already overwhelming mix of emotions.

"He clearly loves his daughter," Wayne said. "I ca
relate to that."

"I… Dad, do you think I'd make a good parent?"

He set the paper down, met her gaze. "The more impo
tant question, darlin', is what do you think?"

"I hadn't given it much thought. This didn't feel like th
right time in my life for that." She was in her early—oka

ne, *mid*-twenties, on her own for the very first time. If she
ad a rare maternal urge, she could borrow Ashley for the
ay. Ronnie had always assumed the normal sequence was
ating, marriage, then children; since she rarely dated,
e'd figured she had years before kids were even a distant
nsideration. "I don't feel ready." That didn't make her a
ad person, did it?

"I'm not sure any parent ever does. Not completely. By the
me we had you, I thought for sure I was, I'd already become
father three times. But the first time I saw a little boy smile
you and realized you'd be dating one day, I panicked and
st *knew* I wasn't ready to be the father of a daughter."

"Lucky for you," she said with a wry smile, "I didn't
ate very often."

He winked at her. "And I appreciate that. Maybe I
ouldn't have worried so much about you, though. If this
IcDeere fellow is any indication, you have good taste."

"Thanks, Dad." There was no reason her dad ever
eeded to know about some of the local bad-boys she'd
und attractive when she was younger. "And thanks for
greeing to let Emily come into the shop Saturday."

"You just make sure she stays out of my way if I'm
orking."

Ronnie smothered a laugh. Even when he tried to sound
uff, there was no mistaking the fact that Wayne Carter
as a big softie. It had taken her moving out of the house
start fully appreciating her family, but Jason McDeere
asn't the only great guy in her life.

AYNE CARTER WAS SMITTEN. As he raced around with the
nall brunette perched on his shoulders—the denim cap

and tiara she insisted on wearing together both knocke
askew—Ronnie could have sworn she heard her father..
giggle? Surely not. Emily's own laughter reverberated of
the concrete. Ronnie leaned against a shelving uni
shaking her head at how quickly Em had wrapped the bi
man around her tiny pinkie finger.

"You don't mind that he's carrying her like that, d
you?" she asked Jason. "He's more careful than he look
I promise." He'd carried Ronnie like that once, and year
later, his grandchildren.

"I'm just worried about how his shoulders and neck ar
going to hold up. Is there a good chiropractor in town?
He turned to Ronnie with a smile that almost made he
forget they weren't alone.

"S-so what did you want to talk to me about?"

He'd made a point of corralling her into the corne
where they could speak with more privacy. "Easter."

She'd braced herself for several possible answers. Tha
wasn't one of them.

Noting her expression, he said, "I'm guessing you haven
talked to Kaitlyn since yesterday. When I picked up Emil
Kaitlyn invited me to spend Easter Sunday with your famil
at your dad's house. She told me I could bite the bullet an
meet all three brothers at once since Will's coming to tow
You and I talked about my meeting your brothers?" h
prompted when Ronnie had yet to show any reaction.

Yeah, they'd talked about it, but Ronnie hadn't bee
rushing to find an opportunity. She glanced to where h
father was carrying Jason's daughter, thought abou
Kaitlyn playing with Emily while Ashley was at scho
yesterday. Her life and Jason's were fast becoming enta

led in ways that sent skitters of anxiety through her. *Slow own, back up the truck!*

"I didn't tell her yes," he said stiffly. "I thanked her for he invitation and told her I'd get back to her. Maybe it's or the best I tell her no. I don't want to intrude."

His disappointment was palpable, and Ronnie loathed erself for having caused it. She'd recently thought how sad was for Emily and Jason that they had no family support earby, yet she begrudged them one afternoon with her own?

"No, no, you should join us!" Did her sudden enthusiasm ound like overcompensation? "The more the merrier."

"More!" Emily echoed as Wayne drew closer to the ther adults.

"Not today," Ronnie interceded. "You and your dad vere leaving soon for lunch and milkshakes, remember?"

At the mention of milkshakes, Emily tried to scramble own.

"Whoa there," Wayne said. "Let me help you so you on't fall, okay?"

"'Kay."

"Whew," Wayne said once he had her feet back on the round. "You're awfully heavy! But I guess that's what I et for carrying around a ten-year-old."

"I'm not ten!"

"Eight?" Wayne guessed. "Wait, don't tell me, twelve."

The child belly-laughed. "I 'bout to turn three."

"Two weeks from today," Jason confirmed proudly. "We ave to decide what kind of cake to buy, kiddo."

"That's an important decision," Wayne agreed gravely. Almost as important as the present list. Do you already now what you want to ask for?"

Emily nodded, her eyes gleaming with excitement. "/
mommy!"

Involuntarily, Ronnie broke the ensuing silence with
sound that was half gasp and half-nervous titter. As a resul
everyone looked at her instead of the little girl. Jason wa
frowning, in contrast to his daughter's expectant smile.

"Coming to my party, Ronnie?" the little girl implore
So far, Ronnie hadn't given a straight answer.

"I'm sure she wouldn't miss it," Wayne quickly assure
his new friend. "And I hear you might be at my house fc
Easter! Maybe your dad would let you open an early present

Resisting the urge to smack her forehead, Ronni
mentally smacked her family instead. Normally, when th
Carters interfered, it was to drive a guy away. Now the
seemed to be conspiring to throw her and Jason togethe
Correction. She stole a glance at the little girl with suc
bright hopes in her eyes. Her, Jason and Emily.

Chapter Ten

Glad that Emily was no longer fearful when she got into a vehicle, Jason buckled his daughter into her booster seat after lunch. He'd barely eaten, but she'd been happily preoccupied with her chocolate milkshake. It would be tough to urge her to eat her meals if she noticed he wasn't touching his own food. He'd lost his appetite, but he felt as though he were on the verge of losing a whole lot more.

I've been a dumb-ass. So blind.

The signs had been there, but he'd naively misread them. When Ronnie had asked the other day about Emily, about the potential dangers of their dating when he had a daughter, he'd been touched that she was concerned about his daughter's feelings. But he now realized that wasn't her only concern. When Emily had made her typically toddler blunt declaration that she wanted a mommy, as if it were no more complicated than wanting ice cream or a toy pony, Ronnie had gone stark white. For a split second, he'd actually thought the pragmatic mechanic might faint on the cement floor of her garage.

Hell. Under different circumstances, he would empathize. Kids were a huge responsibility. He still had his

nervous moments, and he'd had nine months to prepare fo
impending parenthood. He and Ronnie hadn't even bee
on nine *dates*. Yet, he couldn't put Ronnie's feelings—
even his own—above his daughter's. If Ronnie wasn't sur
she wanted Em in her life, then he couldn't be in Ronnie'

He glanced at Emily in the rearview mirror, noticing th
way the sunlight through the window made the jewels o
her tiara shine. Pretty, but fake and ultimately fragile.

"You want to see if Zoë can come over and play this af
ternoon?" Given his current mood, their across-the-stre
neighbor might be a better companion for tea parties an
make-believe.

Emily sighed. "Zoë has a mommy. And Ashley. An
B'linda," she said, referring to Coach Hanover's daughte

"I know, sweet pea." *And I'm so sorry.*

"I want a mommy," she said pleadingly.

He chose his words carefully. "You do have
mother…but she doesn't live with us. You remember th
pictures I've shown you?"

"Mommies should live with kids."

In a perfect world? God, yes. He tried a different tac
"What kinds of things would you like to do with
mommy? Read stories, play dolls, finger-paint? Mayb
there's something *I* can do with you."

She didn't answer. He wasn't sure whether to feel dis
couraged or relieved.

As they turned into their subdivision, she commente
"Ronnie's pretty."

He wished he could believe his daughter was just makin
conversation and not a suggestion. Maybe in this case,
segue was better than trying to explain the complexities

adult relationships…especially since *he* could barely wrap his mind around them. "It'll be nice if she can come to your party, but plenty of other people will be there, too. Wanda and Zoë, the Hanovers, Maggie and her son Nathan…"

"Miss Kaitlyn and Ashley?"

"Uh-huh." Emily had promptly invited them after playing at their house Friday. It hadn't bothered him at the time—he'd actually looked forward to becoming closer to Ronnie's family—but now he questioned the wisdom of spending two consecutive weekends with them. "And Miss Nina said she'd drop by, too!"

He would take Emily to the party store, let her pick out decorations, flip through a picture book of possible cakes at the bakery and generally make a fuss. What were the chances that if he showered enough affection on her and made the event festive enough that his three-year-old would overlook being denied the one thing she'd truly wanted? Pathetic, he admonished himself as he hit the button for the electric garage door opener, but at least it gave him a temporary plan.

"Daddy? Can I get a strawberry cake?"

"For your party? Absolutely!" He exhaled in a gust of grateful relief. "*That* I can do."

RONNIE WAS HEADED FOR the front door when it opened. Lola Ann stepped inside, looking nervous but otherwise pretty in a light blue sweater that gently highlighted her curves, and a flowing skirt.

"Hey." Ronnie gave her friend an admiring smile. "Someone's been shopping! I'm headed out to Ashley's game. Want to come with me?" Her niece's spring softball season had just started, with Danny assisting as coach for the team.

Lola Ann smiled, but her eyes darted anxiously around the office. "Tell her I said good luck. But I'm not actually here to see you. I, uh, thought I'd swing by and see if your brother had dinner plans tonight."

That explained the outfit and stylishly braided hair. "Sorry, he's working on a new site just outside town limits. Maybe you can catch up with him at his place later?"

Grimacing, Lola Ann fidgeted with the neckline of her sweater. "Coming here was one thing. I'm not sure I'm up for just accosting him at his house."

Ronnie paused at Danny's desk to grab a memo pad and scrawl her brother's number. "Well, if you decide you're brave enough to call him, here."

"Thanks. I think."

"You'll never know if you don't try." Her own advice haunted her as she walked to her car. Was the same true in her case? Maybe instead of subtly distancing herself from Jason, she should—

No, generally speaking, being a parent wasn't something you got to do for a sixty-day, money-back trial period. She could do more damage than good—to Emily, Jason and to herself. The truth she'd been putting off was inescapable. Next time she saw Jason, she should make her position clear. It would be best if they were friends. *Just* friends.

Tears stung her eyes, but she wiped them away as she drove toward the park. She'd fixed a smile in place by the time she climbed the bleachers toward the seat Kaitlyn was saving. Down on the field, the game had already started. Ronnie grinned at the way Danny was encouraging the girls. Who would have guessed any of her brothers, responsible early in her life for pulling her hair when their parents weren't looking and telling her scary stories, would turn out to be a great dad?

"You've only missed a minute or two," Kaitlyn said as Ronnie sat next to her. "Ashley's batting next."

The girl stepped up for her turn; Ronnie heard the faint *thwack* as the ball connected. It landed only a few feet in front of her, but while members of the opposing team were crashing into one another in their haste to get it, Ashley managed to run to first base. Kaitlyn called out praise for her daughter's efforts, and Ronnie put two fingers in her mouth and let out an ear-splitting whistle.

Kaitlyn rubbed her ear. "Let me guess, your brothers taught you how to do that?"

Ronnie nodded. Why was it she'd learned that stuff so well? In theory, she even knew how to hot-wire a car, though she'd never tested the capability. Yet when her mother had tried to teach her how to decorate a cake, thread a sewing machine, or knit… If she'd had more time with her mother, would Ronnie have eventually got the hang of those arts, or was she simply not that kind of daughter? She knew Sue had loved her, but it must have been a bit disappointing, to finally have a daughter after three boys only to have that daughter chase after her big brothers to be included on guy outings.

Keeping her eyes on the field below, Kaitlyn sighed. "It's too bad there aren't any games next weekend. I understand why they aren't having them, with the holiday and people traveling, but it would have been fun if her uncle Will could have come to see her."

Ronnie slanted a glance at her sister-in-law. "About next

weekend. I was a little surprised to learn that you'd invited Jason and Emily to have dinner with us."

Kaitlyn arched an eyebrow, faintly challenging. "I was a little surprised to learn that you *hadn't*. This is their first big holiday in town since they lost Sophie. You of all people must know how hard that is. Besides, you're seeing him, aren't you? I heard it was getting serious."

"Heard from whom?"

Kaitlyn lowered her voice. "Heather Lynn Jacob saw him at the grocery store. Buying condoms."

Heat flooded Ronnie's face. It was probable that he'd meant them for her, and oh, how she wanted to put them to good use. "People in this town need to get a life," she mumbled.

"I'm not judging—you're an adult, and he's seriously cute. It's just that I didn't think the invitation would be a big deal. Lola Ann attends so many family dinners we could give her the honorary last name Carter."

Ronnie choked on her laughter, thinking that her friend might not mind making that name change more than honorary. "Well, Lola Ann's spending Easter with her parents, so she won't be there."

"Emily can sit at the kids table with Ashley and Will's boys. She'll have a blast dyeing eggs with them."

No doubt. And that scared Ronnie. Kaitlyn saw this as no more than open hospitality; would the little girl see the afternoon as encouragement of her dreams?

"Emily turns three soon."

Kaitlyn nodded. "She invited Ash to her party."

"And did she tell you what she's hoping to get for her birthday? A mommy."

"Poor baby. And poor Jason. I know he's doing the best he can, but it probably still doesn't feel adequate."

"I really care about this guy," Ronnie confessed miserably.

"But? That sounds like a *good* thing…unless you aren't crazy about Emily."

"It's not how I feel about her, it's how I feel about the whole package. About me." Becoming a mother. She almost shuddered, which couldn't be a good sign.

"Oh." Kaitlyn straightened, understanding and chagrin dawning on her face. "You aren't sure you want to keep seeing him romantically, are you? And I up and invited him to spend time with your entire family. Wow, I stink at the helpful sister-in-law role. I'm sorry, Ronnie."

"It's okay." She was glad to find she meant it. "I admit, I was thrown when he mentioned it, but you were acting out of kindness. And Jason can use that right now. He's insanely grateful for you helping out with Emily on Friday."

"It was fun. I'm happy to be out of the potty-training days and have a few more hours of the day to myself with Ashley in school, but they change so fast. It's kind of nice to revisit that age with someone else's kid. I'm keeping her a couple of days next week, too." Kaitlyn bit her lip. "If that's okay?"

Ronnie's laugh was humorless. "I may have to break up with him, but that doesn't mean the rest of the town should, my relatives included."

The question was, how would Ronnie bear constantly seeing him around town, knowing what they'd almost shared?

SINCE RONNIE HAD TO STAY home on Tuesday—she was awaiting an appliance repairman who'd sworn to be there sometime between 9:00 a.m. and July—she'd planned to sleep in that morning. Unfortunately, a ringing phone thwarted this plan shortly after seven.

"Hello?"

"Ronnie, it's Kaitlyn." Her sister-in-law sounded upset. Not hysterical, but definitely more frazzled than most people were before the day had even started.

"Everything okay?" Ronnie asked, sitting up in bed.

"Ashley's got some kind of stomach flu. Started throwing up around three in the morning and hasn't stopped."

Ugh. "Sorry to hear that. Is there anything I can do to help?" She'd only attempted Sue Carter's chicken soup recipe once, and Devin had claimed it made him even sicker.

"Well, I was supposed to babysit Emily, but I don't want to expose her to a virus. I called Jason at six-thirty and he's already called Wanda Spencer, who's getting a cavity filled midmorning, and Caren Hanover, who's chaperoning on her daughter's field trip today. Right now he's trying to reach his grandmother's old friend Adele. But she's eighty-two. She loves Emily, but Jason's afraid an entire day with her might be a bit much."

Ronnie smothered a yawn, processing the unspoken request. "So Jason wants to know if I'll watch Emily today?"

Kaitlyn paused. "Actually, he very specifically didn't mention you. Maybe that's just because he assumed you'd be working today. Since I knew about the stove…"

Sunday night, Ronnie had decided to be ambitious and cook herself some spaghetti. Yet when she'd tried to turn off the burner, the blue flame had refused to die. After calling Danny to troubleshoot, she'd finally wrestled the oven away from the wall—praying silently that she

wouldn't find anything skittering behind the appliance—
to disconnect the gas. A professional was coming out today
to fix the problem so that she didn't have to worry about a
gas leak next time she tried to cook.

Although, frankly, she'd learned her lesson. *If I'd only
microwaved...*

"Ronnie? You will help, won't you?"

She sighed. "Of course I will. Do you want to call Jason
and tell him, or should I?"

"THANK YOU." IT WAS THE third time he'd said it, and Jason
was barely in the front door. Emily, however, had barreled
past, a pink, denim-capped blur sporting a princess
backpack and intent on checking out Ronnie's environment. "We really appreciate this."

"No problem. I had to stay home today, anyway. Might
as well have some company, right?" But her attempted
cheer sounded flat in her own ears.

"Ronnie." He tipped her chin up with his finger, his expression solemn but nonaccusatory. "We need to talk, don't
we?"

She swallowed, blaming herself enough for both of
them. "I guess we do. I wish we didn't, though."

Silently echoing the sentiment, he leaned forward so
that his forehead barely rested against hers. Even that brief,
platonic contact—bringing him so close to her—left her
starved for more, conjuring memories of the only other
time he'd been to her house. The night of the Spring Fling,
when it seemed that they were at the start of something new
and wonderful.

Something that was ending before it begun.

"You should get to work," she said. It was the truth, not a stalling tactic. Besides, they couldn't stand in her entryway discussing the complicated parenthood aspect of the situation when Emily herself might dash between them at any second.

Jason called his daughter back to say goodbye and handed over a duffel bag to Ronnie, with snacks, juice boxes and a change of clothes he'd packed. Then he knelt to kiss Emily and tell her to behave.

As he stood, the little girl asked, "Kiss Ronnie, too? Because you carrot her!"

"Care about her," he corrected absently, his gaze locked on Ronnie's.

A hot shiver went through her. Trying to repress a keen sense of loss, she knew she couldn't stand even a brief peck right now.

Instead, she flashed Emily an overbright smile. "I *might* have a bottle of nail polish around here that hasn't completely dried up. If I can find it, do you want me to paint your toes?"

Amid Emily's enthusiasm for this plan, Jason left. Ronnie tried not to flinch when he pulled the door shut behind him. Even though he was coming back that afternoon, the sound of the door closing felt very much like goodbye.

JASON WAS IN THE MIDST of dissecting a Greek tragedy—entirely appropriate to his mood—when an office aide interrupted his second period with a note. There was a woman waiting in the office who hoped he could come speak with her between classes. He frowned at the pink slip. His mind, of course, went to Ronnie, recalling the last

ime she'd surprised him at school. Part of him wished it
vere her today.

But the only reason she would have come was Emily;
f there was an emergency involving his daughter, the
iote would have said so. No, this was probably a parent
vho wanted a quick moment of his time. Just because
Ronnie was his current mental default mode didn't mean
inything. Everything reminded him of her. Hell, he could
it next to another vehicle at a red light and wonder if
he'd worked on it.

It isn't fair. Then again, he and Ronnie already had
eason to understand life *wasn't* always fair. People
ouldn't always control their circumstances, merely their
esponses. He planned to be gracious and move forward.
After all, this time with Ronnie had proved one thing—
ie'd been wrong all those times he'd insisted to Hank
Hanover or Wanda Spencer that he had no interest in
lating, in sharing his life with someone. Maybe, after he'd
;iven himself some time to get over Ronnie, he'd let Hank
et him up on a date. He didn't want to be permanently
lone, and Emily certainly wanted a mother.

Keeping one eye on the clock, he wound the lecture
lown a few moments before the bell rang. "If you guys
iaven't read the assigned material yet, tonight's your last
hance. Quiz tomorrow!"

This announcement was met with the predictable groans.

His tone was dry as he pointed out, "Hey, at least I
varned you. Next time it could be a pop quiz."

They stopped complaining so fast that he almost
aughed. As the students filed out of the room, Jason
ollowed, dodging the gathering crowds near lockers to

make his way to the front of the school. There, he opene
the door and turned toward the receptionist.

"I received a—"

"Jason." The soft voice behind him was hauntingl
familiar, yet he couldn't really believe that she'd be ther
when he turned.

He moved in slow motion, the moment taking on
strange dreamlike quality. *Or should that be nightmare*
God, it was really her. She'd become even more beautifu
over time, if that were possible. Yet attraction was the ver
last thing he felt for her.

"Hello, Isobel."

Chapter Eleven

Ronnie's morning passed easily enough. She and Emily blew soap bubbles in the yard, colored pictures and watched an animated movie Ashley had given Ronnie one Christmas. After lunch, however, Emily clearly began to get restless.

Initially, Ronnie had planned to attempt repairing her garbage disposal today, but Emily peppered her with questions that made it hard to focus on the do-it-yourself instructions. Instead, Ronnie ended up sitting on the floor of her kitchen giving Emily a summary of what different tools were called and what each did. The little girl absorbed the information quickly, obviously bright. Ronnie felt a surge of pride she hadn't earned. Jason was solely responsible for how well his daughter was turning out.

Unfortunately, Emily wanted to try her hand at using all the tools. Ronnie winced at the thought of the toddler working a drill, and the hammer was way too heavy for her to safely wield.

"I tell you what," Ronnie suggested, "why don't you bring me that storybook from your backpack? We can read in my room. You could even take a nap on my bed if you wanted."

"No nap!"

Well, it had been worth a try, although, in retrospect maybe Ronnie had gone for the subtle approach. They adjourned to the bedroom with the large storybook.

Emily pointed at a frame Ronnie had hung up that weekend, an oversize mahogany square divided into lots of different-size windows. "Ashley!"

"Yep." Ronnie tapped the glass. "And this one here is Ashley when she was just a baby, younger than you."

Emily was equally delighted to pick out Wayne and "Miss Kaitlyn," along with Danny in their engagement photo. But she was unsure who Devin or Will were and stared at Ronnie quizzically when she got to one with Sue.

"That's me when I was about Ashley's age. With my mom. She's gone now," Ronnie explained, heading off possible awkward questions on Easter Sunday.

"Like my mommy?"

Ronnie's throat felt thick. "Not exactly. My mom's in heaven, like your Gran."

Emily nodded, then sidled closer to pat Ronnie's hand.

A damp laugh escaped Ronnie, the irony of being comforted by this small, equally motherless, girl. She pulled Em close in a half hug. Then they climbed onto the bed. Ronnie couldn't deny a vague feeling of coziness, leaning on the mound of pillows with Emily's warm body snuggled trustingly against hers.

"All right, let's see what stories we have in here!" She scanned the index. Cinderella—a girl whose real mother dies, followed by her father, consigning Cindy to become an unpaid maid in her own home. *Not my idea of a fair tale.* Snow White—a girl's natural mother dies, eventually subjecting the heroine to the evil whims of a jealous step-

mother, who drives her out of her home and into domestic
servitude for seven little men.

Who the hell writes these things? Granted, Cinderella
and Snow White eventually ended up with their respective
Prince Charmings, but, today Ronnie didn't think she could
bring herself to utter the princess's famous "and they lived
happily ever after" endings.

Ronnie took a deep breath. "How do you feel about
Three Billy Goats Gruff?"

What did it say about her life that a scary troll repeatedly leaping out to eat up the other characters seemed like
the least traumatic option?

JASON FIGURED THERE WASN'T a person alive who hadn't
scripted at least one imaginary scene for running into an
ex. Depending on the daydreamer's mood, these scenes
could range from passionate reconciliation to a belated
opportunity to apologize or that coolest of revenges,
running into an ex you're truly over while you look great
and are at the height of success. He'd pictured Isobel
knocking on the front door of their home, tearfully apolo-
gizing and cradling their baby to her as she promised never
to leave them again.

But he'd never pictured Isobel just showing up one
day at his place of work; the baby he'd hoped she would
one day want to cradle as her own was about to become
a preschooler. He sat with his ex-wife at the long bank
of blue-vinyl-padded chairs used for those waiting to see
the principal, school nurse or guidance counselor. He
was torn between asking Isobel what the hell she was
doing here and demanding to know, for their daughter's

sake, what had taken so long. Instead, he simply state
the mundane.

"My third-period class starts in about five minutes."

She nodded. In the past, she'd worn her dark brown hai
quite long, hiding her face behind it or twisting the end
whenever she was anxious. Now it was a short, layere
shag that framed her delicate features. She kept her finger
firmly interlocked in her lap.

"It was inconsiderate for me to show up here, but
wanted to make sure I found a way to see yo
without…Emily being around." Pain flashed through he
eyes when she spoke her daughter's name. "That kin
of ambush seemed unfair to you and potentially upse
ting for her."

"You could have called," he pointed out. His grand
mother's number was the same it had been since before h
met Isobel; he'd merely had it transferred to his name.

"I was afraid that if I gave you a warning, you woul
refuse to see me," she admitted in a near whisper. "Woul
refuse to let me see her."

Her confession, no matter how earnest, pissed him off-
since when had he tried to deny her access to her child?
had been Isobel's choice to leave. And, yet, even as th
righteous anger swelled, on some level, he didn't want he
spending time with Emily. Their daughter was especiall
vulnerable right now, desperately wanting a mother, an
he had a feeling that, after Easter and Em's birthday part
neither of them would be seeing much of Ronnie anymor
If Isobel waltzed back into Emily's life, then turned aroun
just as capriciously…

Hell. He plowed a hand through his hair. "I can me

you somewhere for lunch in about an hour, but you can't wait here."

Stealing a piece of paper out of the copier tray, he drew her a map for Tennessee Tacos—it would be less crowded at lunch than Adam's Ribs or the Sandwich Shoppe, but he felt a twinge of guilty unreality. The Mexican restaurant had been the site of his first date with Ronnie; he never could have imagined returning there with his ex-wife.

Doubting his ability to get through a coherent lecture for his next class, he let them work on group projects for the end of the semester instead. Students turned their desks to face one another in little clusters of three and four and the buzz of multiple concurrent conversations rivaled the buzz in his skull, the static of memories and doubts and questions he couldn't yet answer. He sat at his desk, trying to look as if he were grading, when really he was just trying to make it through the next forty minutes. Almost without realizing it, he'd pulled his cell phone from his pocket.

I want to talk to Ronnie.

It was a bizarre realization, how close he still felt to her despite her tacit admission this morning that they wouldn't be dating anymore. That the one memorable night they'd shared would be their last. Bitter disappointment caused him to grind his teeth as he pushed away the images of the short-lived happiness.

Still, Ronnie was there for him. From that first lunch, when she'd been so easy to talk to, coaxing his burdens from his shoulders, through today, when she was babysitting a kid who adored her even if it was personally awkward for her. Ronnie was the kind of solid, steadfast woman he doubted Isobel could become no matter how many years passed. His wife had been beautiful, musically gifted and mercurial.

What would he say to Isobel?

By the time he left the school to meet her, he'd decided that he should just let her do the talking. After all, if she'd shown up in Joyous after all this time, she obviously had some things she wanted to get off her chest.

She was already waiting inside, sitting in a booth in the back corner of the restaurant. Had she requested something that afforded them a bit more privacy, or had he simply got lucky in this one meaningless instance?

At his approach, she glanced up. "You look good, Jace. You always did, but now…you look good."

"Thank you." He could respond in kind, but he wasn't here to trade complimentary small talk. "I don't mean to sound rude, but what are you doing here?"

She fiddled with the straw in her glass of ice water. "Her birthday's coming up."

"Emily," he said insistently. He'd seen what it cost her to say the name earlier, but avoiding it struck him as a kind of distancing. Didn't she think she'd already put enough distance between herself and her child?

Isobel's eyes flashed with anger. Not at him, he realized as she spoke, but herself. "Dammit, I know what her name is. I picked it out, remember? Her name, the sound of her laugh, wondering what she looks like with each passing day…they've all haunted me."

How sad for you. He could have said it, flippantly, cruelly, but in truth, it *was* sad for her, all that she'd missed. Intellectually, he knew her condition wasn't something she'd elected. Part of him even acknowledged that Emily

night have been better off with one parent during her for-
native first years than two parents, one of whom was emo-
ionally unstable. Yet there was still too much anger inside
or the hurt Isobel had caused Em for him to magnani-
mously declare the woman forgiven.

A waitress came to take their orders, and Jason picked
omething at random. Food was the least of his current
concerns.

Once they were alone, Isobel recounted, "On Emily's
rst birthday, I felt physically crippled. I couldn't get out of
ed. I wanted to call her, but I couldn't stop sobbing. I figured
ot hearing from me was better than hearing from a neurotic
ness. It was soon after that I went looking for a new thera-
ist, tried to pull myself together with varying degrees of
access. I almost called you on her second birthday, but I was
aralyzed with fear. What if another woman answered the
hone? What if Emily didn't even know who I was? Of
ourse she doesn't. She was too young."

"I've shown her pictures," he said stiffly. "It's been dif-
cult to figure out what to say about your…absence, but I
ever pretended you didn't exist."

She reached across the table, squeezing his hand.
Thank you, Jason."

Had there really been a time when this woman's touch
nt sparks through him? Now what he felt was mostly her
esperation, her sorrow. It took physical effort not to dis-
ntangle from her fingers.

Perhaps she sensed his feelings, though. She tucked her
ands into her lap, beneath the table. "I just knew I couldn't
t one more birthday pass, one more year go by, without
eeing my baby. That is, if you'll let me?"

"And then what?" he asked without rancor. "This isn't n being vindictive, it isn't about us. It's about what's best f Em. How does this play out in your head? You show up wit a giant pink teddy bear on her birthday, hug her and wis her a nice life, then disappear once again into the horizon Or have you fantasized stepping in to finally be a parent? have to be honest, I'd fight you on split custody. She need more stability in her life, and I think we can find it in Joyous

"No, I'm definitely not ready for any kind of custody Isobel agreed too quickly.

Instead of reassuring him, her words, paradoxicall incensed him. Why was his life littered with women wh didn't want his daughter?

"Jason, I know you're doing a wonderful job with her—

"You *don't* know that! You have very little idea of wh her life has been like and until now haven't seemed to gi a damn one way or the other. For all you know, I've bee a terrible father, shuttling her off on sitters while I date string of faceless rebound women."

Her sigh of exaggerated patience made him feel like an as

He pinched the bridge of his nose. "No, of course haven't been doing anything of the sort. But I'm not su I'm Father of the Year, either. It hasn't been easy."

"I don't know to whom I owe the greater apology," s said, her bearing quietly regal. The composure and short hair made her truly look like a different woman than the o he'd married. A self-possessed stranger. "You or Emily."

"I appreciate the sentiment, but you didn't need to con here to say you're sorry." The romantic part of their pa was done and gone. "We just need to decide what to c about Emily, what, if anything, to tell her."

He could ask the girl if she wanted to see her mother, but given all her hints of late, he knew the answer would be a resounding yes. Emily was too young to understand the possible fallout of the decision, the way she'd feel when Isobel left. Again.

Leaning away from the table to make room for the waitress to set down hot plates, Isobel said, "I should tell you… I'm considering joining the Chattanooga symphony."

Chattanooga? The city was an improbable commute to Joyous, but it was certainly close enough for weekend visits or showing up for special occasions in your daughter's life. So Isobel *had* given this some thought and hadn't just shown up on a birthday-induced emotional whim. He felt oddly proud of her; at the same time his head spun dizzily. If she'd planned this to be an aberration, he would have easily told her she couldn't interact with Emily—maybe watched her play at the park from a careful distance, but there would be no raising the girl's hopes. The fact that Isobel was taking more responsibility seemed promising, yet also added another layer of complications.

They made it through the rest of the meal with civil, though awkward, conversation. She seemed more like a blind date than someone he'd once known intimately. Maybe he hadn't. Afterward, he gave her his cell phone number and wrote down her room at the bed-and-breakfast. She was planning to stay for at least another night, then go to Chattanooga to talk to the symphony people and apartment hunt. Her hope was to come back the weekend of Emily's birthday, but he wasn't ready to promise that yet.

Would the party be a good first time for mother and daughter to interact? On the one hand, it seemed like it

should be a private moment. On the other, having othe
people around, in a celebratory atmosphere, might take of
some of the pressure.

Unable to help himself, he dialed Ronnie's number. H
felt too emotionally raw from the lunch to discuss it wit
anyone just yet, but even the sound of her voice would b
calming before he walked into his next class.

"Hello?" She sounded breathless, and Emily wa
laughing in the background.

In spite of everything else, he smiled. "It's Jason. Hov
are you holding up?"

"I wouldn't say no to an energy boost, but we're havin
a good time. Aren't we, Emily?"

"Yes, yes, yes!"

"Glad to hear it. I should be there by four-thirty to get her.

"Feel free to walk in and shout out a hello." Ronni
continued in that same cheerfully casual voice he didn'
quite buy, not after the sheen of tears he'd glimpsed tha
morning. "The doorbell sounded like a dying goos
when I moved in and now it's given out altogether. Fror
the back of the house, we almost didn't hear the repair
man knock."

"Walk in, give a shout. Got it."

There was a pause. "What about you—how are yo
holding up?"

Whether she asked because she could hear the strain i
his voice or because of their exchange that morning, h
didn't know. The temptation to unload everything wa
strong, but it wasn't a conversation he could cram into th
next few minutes. "I'll be okay. Can I say hi to the kiddo?

"Of course."

After a few seconds of background noise, his daughter came on the line. "Hi, Daddy."

Hearing her voice, thinking what it would mean to her to know her mother was right here in Joyous, caused a lump in his throat. *God, just let me make the right decisions for her.* "I love you, sweet pea."

"Love you, too, Daddy. Bye-bye!" Click.

No doubt he'd been unceremoniously disconnected so that she could return to whatever fun she was having with Ronnie. He couldn't blame her. He wanted the balm of Ronnie's company right now, too.

As a literature teacher, he really should be appreciating the irony of the situation more: the erstwhile wife and mother had returned, yet she was no longer the woman he wanted in his life.

SINCE RONNIE HAD NEVER looked after Emily before, she didn't know whether Jason always called to check on his daughter. Maybe it was simply routine, something good parents did. But there had been something in his voice...

"Ronnie, come look at my picture!"

Snapping out of her thoughts, Ronnie came to the kitchen table to praise the girl's artistic efforts. After spending so many hours with her, it barely registered that most of Emily's *R*s and *L*s came out as *W*s. This morning, he'd had to ask Emily to repeat quite a few things when the little girl had been excited and speaking quickly; when the repairman had been here and Emily had been asking him questions, he'd shot Ronnie more than one quizzical *translation, please?* glance. Ronnie was glad to be getting the hang of it.

"That's beautiful," Ronnie told the girl, looking at the bright profusion of marker across the white computer paper. "I like your use of color. In fact…you want to help me with something?"

Emily began bouncing in her chair with excitement. Ronnie tried to think back to Ashley at this age—were all kids this age so easy to please? If so, why did people whine about "terrible twos" and "tyrannical threes?"

"I want to paint my hallway," she said. "Maybe you'd like to help?"

There was a coat closet at the end of the hall. Ronnie hadn't planned to paint inside that, but there was no reason the girl couldn't. It's not as though anyone was going to be scrutinizing the inner closet walls, and it would allow Emily to have fun while Ronnie actually accomplished something. Her housewarming party was Saturday. It didn't matter if she fixed the doorbell or disposal by then, but she'd love to get some more of the cosmetic stuff done so that her friends could see her new home at its best advantage.

Ronnie had rounded up all the supplies they'd need and was taping plastic over the carpet when the phone rang again.

Emily looked up. "Daddy?"

"Maybe." Although he should be back in class by now. She picked up the remote control and zapped the television on to a child-friendly program while she answered the phone. "Hello?"

"Hey, Red. I heard you're on babysitting duty because Ashley's feeling puny today."

"That's right." Although it didn't seem like something her brother would call to talk about. "What's up?"

"You know I love you, right?"

She stared at the receiver. "Okay, random proclamations like that make me think you're dying or something. Please tell me you're not dying."

"No, but if you ever needed me to murder someone on your behalf—"

"Dev!"

He sighed. "I ran into Tennessee Tacos to grab enchiladas-to-go for the guys on my crew. And I saw McDeere. Way in the back, having lunch with some woman I didn't recognize. Real looker, though. Ronnie, the very last thing in the world I want is to hurt you, but I won't tolerate some jerk making a fool of you, either. Whoever she was, McDeere was holding hands with her."

A burst of psychic pain hit, the spiritual version of a debilitating migraine. "Oh."

"This probably seems like an inappropriate time to tell you, but before he shows up this evening to—"

"Thank you for caring, you nosy, overprotective so-and-so, but Jason and I aren't together. We're...friends." Of course, if Jason was already expressing romantic interest in someone else, he'd certainly recovered quickly. "You didn't see them *kissing* or anything, right?"

"If you're just friends, does it matter?"

"Devin Eugene," she growled in warning.

"No, all I saw was some hand-holding, but I was only there for a second. If you want, I can find out if Tami was on shift—"

"Lord, no! Jason's a good guy, entitled to happiness. And privacy. We're not asking some ex-chippie of yours to spy on him."

"Okay. Just trying to help."

"Which I appreciate." *Sort of.* "But stop. Now, if that's all, Emily and I were just about to—"

"Actually." Devin cleared his throat. "There is one other thing I wanted to mention. Well, ask really."

She waited, but no question seemed forthcoming. It was unlike Dev to be hesitant. He was normally an act-first, regret-the-consequences-later kind of guy. Although, he was often able to charm his way out of trouble, so the consequences weren't as much of a hindrance for him as they could be for others.

"Devin, when you work construction, you wear a safety helmet, right? Has anything heavy hit you on the head that I should know about? Or maybe you got a little too much sun today?"

"Smart-ass," he chided affectionately. "And to think I was so worried about your feelings."

"With the Jason thing?"

"With Lola Ann," he corrected, stunning her into silence. "I… Would it be all right with you if I asked her to dinner? I know she's your best friend."

A slow smile broke out over her face, and she pumped her fist in the air. Was it possible he'd seen the light? After all these years of her brothers trying to oversee her love life, she was tickled that one of them was now seeking *her* permission to go on a date.

"I think that's a lovely idea," she told him. "If you get lucky, she might even say yes."

Instead of responding to her teasing tone, he seemed to take her comment seriously. "I hope so."

When she hung up the phone, she found herself mentally crossing her fingers for them. In the past, she'd been judgmental about Devin's unwillingness to get close to anyone. Now, however, considering the bittersweet joys of her brief intimacy with Jason, she had a new perspective. Could she entirely blame Devin for wanting to guard his heart? Still, it looked as if he was open to taking a chance. Surely he wouldn't ask out Ronnie's very best friend, someone close to the entire Carter family, if he were interested in another meaningless fling. Ronnie loved Lola Ann and Devin dearly and found herself hoping that, just maybe, they'd find an eventual happy ending.

Someone should.

Chapter Twelve

Jason stepped inside Ronnie's house and was immediately met with the smell of paint and the slightly tinny sound of upbeat music blaring through a less-than state-of-the-art stereo. "Hello?" He didn't have to go far.

His daughter, wearing a T-shirt that draped off one shoulder and hung practically to her knees was dancing across crinkly plastic in Ronnie's hallway, while Ronnie—her own body swaying slightly to the music—rolled a coat of pale, creamy yellow on the walls.

"Daddy!" Emily saw him first, barreling toward him.

Ronnie straightened self-consciously, then turned off the small radio that sat atop a footstool at the end of the hall. She was wearing a tank top and those white shorts he remembered; a splotch of paint dotted her jaw. Another slashed across the neckline of her top, a lemony smear of temptation, drawing his gaze from the hollow of her throat toward her cleavage. Cleavage he'd explored firsthand. Heat rose inside him, a longing that was probably inappropriate but utterly undeniable.

"You two have been busy," he said.

"I paint!" Emily declared. She was sporting more than

a few spots of yellow herself, although it looked as though the shirt Ronnie had lent her bore the brunt of their artistic endeavor.

"Yep." Ronnie ruffled the girl's hair. "She's been helping me fix the place up. Emily, why don't we get you changed back into your clothes so your dad can take you home?"

"I can do it myself," she said proudly, turning in the direction of Ronnie's bedroom.

Ronnie watched the little girl go, sorry to lose the buffer of her presence. Earlier, when Ronnie had been worried about getting Em's clothes messy, she'd pulled out the smallest shirt she could find for her young friend to borrow. Emily's clothes were neatly folded at the foot of Ronnie's bed.

"Can I get you a glass of iced tea?" She'd rather not watch Jason walk into her bedroom.

"Sure, thanks."

She poured the beverages in silence, wondering what he was thinking and if Devin was right about Jason already being interested in someone else. The thought gave her a pang, although it was tinged with guilt. Didn't she *want* Jason to find eventual happiness, to find the perfect woman who would not only cherish him but his deserving little girl? Glowering at the thought, she set down one glass on the table with enough force to slosh tea over the rim. *Real mature, Ron.*

As she went to the sink to grab a damp cloth, he spoke from behind her. "Isobel's in town."

She froze, feeling her eyes widen to the size of hubcaps. "Isobel, your wife?"

"My ex-wife, yeah."

Good Lord. When Devin said Jason was having lunch with someone, she'd thought maybe another teacher maybe a fellow parent in town, giving him advice on Em

Ronnie sank into her chair in a daze. "When—why…?"

"Trust me, I had the same questions. She caught me completely off guard by showing up at the school."

"Wow." If she was this flummoxed, she couldn't begin to imagine how he felt.

"She wants to see Emily, spend her birthday with her." He looked across the table, his gaze ravaged with question she couldn't possibly answer.

But she felt compelled to say something. "Are you okay? Was it…painful seeing her?"

"Uncomfortable. And confusing." At the sound of foot steps in the plastic-lined hallway, he broke off, both of then drinking their tea silently as Emily dashed into the room

"Ready!"

Ronnie looked down at the grinning child and wa shocked to feel a wave of protectiveness. She knew how thrilled Emily would be at the thought of gaining a mother she just hoped Isobel's coming to Joyous didn't inadver tently hurt the girl. *Or her father.*

Jason rose. "Thank you for the tea."

"You're welcome. Let me know if there's anything els I can do." Would he take her up on that? She found tha she sincerely wanted to be his friend. It wasn't enough, an it would sting like hell when he did start dating someon else, but she cared about the McDeeres. That wasn't some thing she could simply turn off like a faucet.

Although, her heart might hurt less if it were.

"I STILL CAN'T BELIEVE IT!" Lola Ann fumed as she tossed pretzels into the cart.

Ronnie didn't feel right discussing the details of Jason's private life in public, so thus far, the conversation while they shopped for tonight's party had focused on the play-by-play of Lola Ann's Friday-night date. With Devin.

"I thought everything went so well," her friend said, uncertainty underscoring her tone as she grabbed another bag. It landed in the basket with a crinkle of plastic and crunch of shifting pretzels. "To be honest, Ronnie, I thought it was one of the best dates I'd ever…but then, nothing! He might as well have shook my hand, for crying out loud!"

"Um, Lola Ann, I think four party-size bags of pretzels is plenty." She reached into the cart. "Actually, *two* is probably plenty. Tell you what, I'll stock, you vent. Just remember your promise. This is my brother you're talking about, so no details that might ook me out."

"No worries there. I can't give you any intimate details *because nothing happened.*" Lola Ann grimaced. "He's supposed to be a fast worker. A girl hears stories."

Ronnie laughed despite herself, steering past the popcorn and toward the soft drinks. "So what, you wanted to be one of the many? Maybe this is Dev's way of showing you that you're special, different from anyone else he's dated."

"Maybe." Lola Ann was silent for a second. "I don't want to be one of the horde, but…I really wanted to kiss him, Ronnie."

I know the feeling. Ronnie could barely be in the same room with Jason without wanting to touch him. Sensual touches, comforting touches, even just the freedom to smooth his hair when he'd tunneled his fingers through it once too often. But she'd given up that freedom when she'd made the conscious choice to keep things platonic between them. It said something about the bond they shared that even without discussing her misgivings in detail, he seemed to understand.

"What if he's not really attracted to me?" Lola Ann asked. "I feel like a nerd admitting this, especially to you, but for months now, I've had this fantasy—"

"Lola Ann!" Ronnie clapped her hands over her ears, the shopping cart veering slightly as she let go of it.

Her friend laughed. "Not that kind of fantasizing. At least, not *only* that kind. It's just that as long as he didn't know how I felt and hadn't rejected me, there was still the possibility, you know? Then he finally asked me out. If after that, he wasn't attracted to me, then now I've lost even the possibility."

Ronnie thought about the way Devin's voice had sounded on the phone when he'd called to let her know he wanted to ask out Lola Ann. "Trust me, I don't think that's the issue."

Thinking of Devin's call led her back to thoughts of Jason having lunch with his ex-wife.

Once they'd purchased the groceries and loaded them into the back of Ronnie's car, she asked, "So have you heard anything about Isobel?" Her understanding was that the woman was gone for now but had stayed in town a few days. Had Jason talked to his daughter about the situation? Ronnie would hate for the girl to overhear a stray piece of gossip and find out the biggest news of her short life through a third party.

"Not much," Lola Ann admitted. "Just that she's…"

"Beautiful? Don't worry, I've already been told that part." The real information she wanted—namely, what Jason had decided to do—she wouldn't be able to get from anyone but him. She'd see him tomorrow at her father's house. If she asked, would he see it as permissible friendly interest or nosy intrusion?

Unbidden, a memory surfaced.

"Can I ask you a question?"

"Ronnie, considering what just happened, you're entitled to get as personal as you want."

She almost groaned. Hopefully, being surrounded by family members and children tomorrow would lessen the potency of seeing Jason. But somehow, she doubted it.

"THAT'S THE WAY TO DO IT, honey!" Coach Hanover applauded his daughter as six of the pins fell. All night, he'd been trying to correct her form and help her aim, but his wife had laughingly chided that Belinda wasn't one of the kids on his team and that there were no medals at stake here tonight.

"We're here to have *fun,* remember?" Caren had asked. She'd pointedly mouthed the word at him in silent reminder as she walked away to take Emily to the ladies' room.

Jason and Em had rented the lane next to the Hanovers, complete with bumpers to help prevent Emily from bowling any gutter balls. His daughter was using the absolute smallest ball available, but even still he had to help her get it started rolling. The important thing, though, as Caren said, was that Emily was having a good time. Jason appreciated the distraction of other people and music playing because, when it was just the two of them at home, he hadn't quite been able to mask his brooding mood this week.

He still hadn't told her about Isobel, although he knew he couldn't put it off much longer.

As Belinda attempted to pick up the spare, Hank came back by Jason, lowering his voice. "Just to let you know, buddy, Caren's got a friend she wants you to meet."

Jason groaned. "Are we going to coincidentally run into her at the alley and invite her to join us?"

"No, nothing that manipulative. She'll probably ask you about it later, and you want to have your counter-argument ready." Hank smiled proudly. "The woman's more stubborn than a bulldog. And your old not-having-the-time-or-interest standby isn't going to fly anymore. Seems like every time I turn around, someone in town's talking about either you and your girlfriend or you and your wife."

"How odd." Jason scowled. "Especially since I have neither."

"You know what I mean."

Though few people had had the guts to ask Jason directly about her, people had noticed Isobel's presence at the bed-and-breakfast. She was the kind of woman who tended to cause a stir—especially when she dropped by the high school and was seen having lunch with him not long after Ronnie had accompanied him to the Spring Fling. Jeez, he was beginning to feel as if his social life was as complicated and "scandalous" as some of his students' appeared to be.

The coach took a swig of root beer, his expression softening as he set the plastic cup down. "So, what did happen with that cute little redhead? Her family's been here forever. Her brothers were cutups in school, but all in all, the Carters are real decent people. It was sad as hell when Sue passed. Ronnie's due for some happiness. And, don't mind my sayin' so, y'all looked pretty happy at the Fling."

"We were," Jason said simply. He wished she was here with them tonight, in his arms, cheering for Emily's attempts, chatting with Caren, laughing at Jason's inability to knock down more than three pins at a time. It was if he'd been living in black and white before she came along, briefly bringing his existence into glorious color. Returning to the status quo was difficult.

Maybe I shouldn't.

Maybe he should keep moving forward, tell Caren that he'd meet this friend. But he didn't want some friend of Caren's. He wanted to grab Ronnie by the shoulders tomorrow and tell her that they were great together, that he was crazy about her, that Emily was crazy about her and that, furthermore, he knew *she* was crazy about them. That had to mean something! Didn't it?

He thought he'd been prepared to walk away from Ronnie, but earlier this week, he'd seen how great she was with his kid. Every day since, Emily had remembered some anecdote she wanted to share about her day at Ronnie's house. Maybe Ronnie was only nervous because she'd lost her own mother so young; maybe she doubted her abilities for want of a role model. If that were the case, they could figure it out together. Both of Jason's parents were living, but he still found himself second-guessing half of his decisions. Maybe instead of bowing out of their nascent relationship so easily, he should have shown more patience.

Across the alley, he saw Emily skipping back toward them, Caren keeping pace with the little girl.

Jason put a hand on Hank's shoulder, stalling the man from taking his turn. "Tell your wife I'm not ready. Not yet."

Tomorrow was Easter Sunday. What were the odds of a miracle? That might be what it took to get Ronnie to see herself the way he did.

DANNY AND KAITLYN HAD TO cancel because their sitter had caught the flu that was going around, but it looked as if everyone else Ronnie had invited would be able to make her party. Lola Ann was there first, of course, helping her arrange party trays of snacks. Treble and Keith Caldwell showed up next, bearing a basket of items Treble said were supposed to bring good fortune in Ronnie's new home. Devin arrived, looking crisp in a white button-down shirt and dark jeans and eliciting a blushing smile of welcome from Lola Ann.

Treble accepted a glass of wine from the hostess glancing meaningfully over the rim of her glass. "Took them long enough, but looks as if they're finally on the right track, doesn't it?"

"Looks like," Ronnie said a bit wistfully.

Bear, shyly accompanying young widow Maggie Cline showed up at the same time as Bill and Charity Sumner and one of Devin's construction co-workers who'd routinely appeared for poker nights when Ronnie lived with her dad.

"You're an absolute doll for inviting us, Ronnie. It's nice to have an adult night out!" Charity shrugged out of the lightweight spring jacket she wore. "Is there somewhere can put this?"

"Right this way." Ronnie led her to the hall closet grinning at the uneven smudges of paint on the back wall—

the coat of yellow extended only three feet high and ignored the first foot of space completely.

She'd need to paint the entire wall before she moved all the eventual contents into the closet, but for some reason, she'd left it this way all week, thinking about how proud Emily had been of her accomplishments, the mischievous gleam in the girl's eyes, the slight swishing sound of her pull-ups as she danced.

"It's a nice little house," Charity complimented. "Reminds me of ours, in a way. Dad's suggested several times that we should look for something bigger, but ours is…cozy. Perfect for the family."

"Well, this one only needs to be perfect for me." A month ago, that would have sounded so liberating. Why, then, did it sound lonely now? She swallowed. "So, does your dad have baby Brooke tonight?"

"Yeah. He's gonna be a problem," Charity said, her voice light and full of affection. "He's crazy about her. And he feels like he wasn't as good a father as he could have been when we were younger, so he sees Brooke as his second chance. If I don't watch him like a hawk, he'll spoil the kid rotten."

Ronnie thought about her own father, giving Emily piggyback rides through the repair bays. Now the image made her smile, although at the time, she'd been uncomfortable. Jason and his daughter had crowded the corners of her life so quickly, endearing themselves not just to her but to family members. Devin and Will had yet to meet the little girl, but it wasn't hard to picture them teasing her good-naturedly or teaching her to skip rocks the way they had with Ronnie, when they were in their more tolerant moods and not trying to chase her away as a pest.

"Earth to Ronnie?" Charity smiled. "It would be a shame if the hostess zoned out of her own party."

Speaking of which, she should go mingle, be hospitable. But she'd pointed out the food and drinks available, and from the rising hum of conversation and laughter in the back rooms—she could easily pick out Treble's voice—nobody missed her just yet.

"Charity, I know how much you love Brooke, so I hope this question doesn't sound insulting, but...do you ever miss your life before?"

Unlike Kaitlyn, who'd been married for more than a decade and had a daughter already in elementary school, Charity was even younger than Ronnie. Also like Ronnie, Charity had lost her mother young, in a car accident, yet not having a mom didn't seem to hamper her own mothering skills.

The blonde smiled gently. "It's not insulting. The glib answer would be to say of course not, that Brooke's the best thing to ever happen to me, etcetera, etcetera. Which, by the way is true. Still, there have been nights when she wouldn't quit crying and I thought I would lose my mind. And there have been times I've snapped at Bill because I felt like I was changing fifteen diapers to every one of his."

Ronnie bit the inside of her cheek to keep from laughing. It was difficult to imagine sweet-tempered Charity snapping at *anyone,* particularly her much-adored husband.

"But it's impossible to imagine my life without her, to remember a time before her, so no, I don't really miss it." Charity's expression turned playfully sly. "Any particular reason you ask?"

Picturing Emily's dark curls and deep laugh, Ronnie returned her friend's smile. "Yeah."

"Then I should also add that when I first found out Bill and I were going to have a baby, I was terrified. And the complications throughout the pregnancy did nothing to reassure me. One of the reasons I've always looked up to Treble is because I've envied my big sister's courage. Parenthood is humbling and scary. I know that doesn't sound like a ringing endorsement, but I promise you, there's never been a day when I've been sorry I had her. It's a scary leap of faith, Ronnie, but there are a lot of rewards at the bottom of the cliff."

Charity made it sound so simple that Ronnie was tempted to jump and hope for the best. But would Jason and Emily be there to catch her, or would a miscalculation on her part end up wounding them all?

Chapter Thirteen

The scene was utter chaos: children chasing one another from room to room, colorful debris littering the kitchen table, Will's wife, Liz, trying in vain to pick up toys strewn through the house and corral the kids upstairs to watch a movie while Kaitlyn and Ronnie cleaned the kitchen. The three Carter brothers, accompanied by Jason, were outside with instructions to stuff and hide all the plastic eggs—at least a dozen for each of the four kids—and Wayne Carter, family patriarch, snored on the couch, louder than a car with a bad exhaust resonator.

Ronnie stood at the sink, washing dishes. She didn't mind the chore. Liz and Kaitlyn, thank heavens, had done the cooking. Through the curtained window, she could see the guys talking and laughing. Occasionally, she'd catch herself leaning forward as if she could hear what they were saying even though there was no chance of that.

"You're not nervous, are you?" Kaitlyn asked. "Your brothers have been on their best behavior with him."

It was true. Since she'd told Kaitlyn and Devin that she didn't think she and Jason were destined to be more than friends, her brothers had taken it easier on him than if she'd introduced him today as her boyfriend. They'd affected a few shudders when he talked about his job of teaching literature, but overall, they really seemed to like him.

Maybe they're not lunkheads after all.

Though Ronnie was rethinking her platonic friendship with Jason, she hadn't shared that news with her brothers. Why jump the gun when she didn't know what Jason's feelings were? The few glimpses she'd caught during dinner had seemed promising, but maybe that was wishful thinking. She needed a few minutes alone with him so they could discuss everything.

Then again, if she managed to get him alone, she might want to put the time toward something other than talking. "Kaitlyn? You kept Emily one day this week, right?"

"Yeah." Kaitlyn reached for a dish towel so she could help dry. "And she spent the whole day trying to convince me to repaint my house."

Ronnie couldn't help laughing at that. "Did you and Jason talk about Isobel?" Since Kaitlyn and Danny were parents, Ronnie thought there was a slight chance Jason might have sought their advice.

"His ex? Just in passing. He guessed that I'd heard the rumors about her being in town and made it clear he didn't want Emily to know yet. I made sure *he* understood that he wouldn't be able to keep it a secret forever, and he told me that he's inviting Isobel to the birthday party."

Well, that was one question answered. "You think that will be a good thing, right? Emily getting a second chance to know her mother?"

Kaitlyn leaned against the counter, pursing her lips. "I know I shouldn't judge, having never walked in the woman's shoes. But I look at Ashley and wonder, how the devil does a mother walk away from her child like that? Still, if she's recovered now and willing to make amends… Despite what happened in the past, if there's a chance Isobel and Emily can have a real mother-daughter relationship in the future, then of course Jason should encourage that. If he didn't, there may come a day when Emily hated him for standing in the way."

Just as the women were putting away the last of the dishes, the back door opened. Jason and Ronnie's two older brothers walked in.

Danny came over to kiss his wife. "Devin forgot his camera and ran over to his place to get it. When he gets back, we'll call the kids down and start the egg hunt."

Kaitlyn tilted her head back to look into her husband's eyes. "Just promise me that this year you kept in mind that none of the hunters are six feet tall!"

"Oh, shoot." Will snapped his fingers. "So putting one up at the base of the chimney was a bad idea?"

Jason had come to the middle of the kitchen and was admiring the wicker basket full of brightly dyed eggs. Ronnie had helped the kids decorate them before lunch, laughing with her niece and nephews, glad to see that Emily, the youngest child present, had no trouble overcoming her shyness to fit in. She was now running around like a crazed banshee just like the Carter children.

Ronnie had given Jason an apologetic smile. "We've ruined her, haven't we?"

"Transformed her, more like. You've been like her fairy godmother."

"I'm not sure I'd do her much good when it comes to

dressing for balls," Ronnie joked, "but I could keep the pumpkin carriage in good working order."

Devin opened the back door, announced that they were a go for Easter eggs, and Danny called up the stairs to the kids. His voice made the floor beneath Ronnie's feet shake, yet her father didn't so much as blink on the couch. Moments later, all the munchkins had been herded downstairs and out the door. Will's boys carried paper sacks, while the girls went slightly more upscale, Ashley using a clean plastic tub that had originally held a gallon of ice cream and Emily tucking her eggs into a rhinestone-studded princess purse.

After twenty-five minutes, the kids had wound down and Will did a quick mental calculation of how many should be left.

"Seven."

"Do you know where any of them are?" Ronnie asked.

Devin snorted. "Four guys hiding fifty eggs, and you think we can remember the exact location of each one?"

By now, the kids each had enough of a hoard that they wanted to go inside to scarf down chocolates, count coins and trade stickers.

"I'll take the kids in so they can sort the loot," Liz offered, "if the rest of the adults want to spread out and hunt up the other eggs."

Danny and Kaitlyn headed for the side yard on the other side of the house; Devin and Will said they'd check the garage.

Ronnie stared up at Jason, thrilled that she'd finally been given that chance to be alone with him but tongue-tied now that it was here. "So, any insight as to where these eggs might be?"

"I know I helped hide them, but honestly my mind was on other things." His tone was as warm as the balmy spring sunshine.

If her brothers had stayed true to form, she knew a few of their hidey-holes. "Follow me."

"Anywhere," he said with a cheeky grin.

"Are you flirting with me?"

"Do you want me to be?"

She stopped, turning to face him. "I— Look!"

He cast a cursory glance over his shoulder. "You'll have to be more specific."

"The bird feeder." There was a wink of fuchsia in one of the trees. "Kids must have missed it because it's above their usual line of sight."

Jason walked over and grabbed the egg. With a boyish grin, he popped the plastic halves apart. "Mmm, chocolate." The foil-wrapped piece of candy was big, almost too large to fit in the egg—a bunny face with two long, straight ears, all of which had softened in the afternoon heat.

Once again, they fell into step with each other, ambling toward the back of the property to check for eggs on the fence line. Jason took a bite of the chocolate and murmured his appreciation.

"You want some?" he asked.

"Yes." Gorgeous man bearing dark chocolate—what woman in the world could resist that?

They came to a halt at the fence. He broke off a piece. "Here." Instead of simply handing it to her, he held the chocolate to her lips.

Ronnie opened her mouth, the silky, bittersweet flavor melting on her tongue. When her lips closed over the tip of is finger, she could have passed it off as an accident, but she new it was deliberate. What had Charity said? *Leap of faith.*

She sucked gently, drawing his finger into her mouth, nd he moaned. He backed her into the fence, intent clear a his eyes as he lowered his face to hers. Their mouths ame together hungrily, and a jolt of lust zigzagged through er. When she kissed him back, his hands went to her hips, auling her up against him. She was drowning in sensation, esperate for him.

"Ronnie." He said the name against her lips, then against er skin as he kissed her neck, her ear, her cheek. "I've nissed you."

It might have sounded silly, considering they'd only een physical with each other the one time, not so long ago, ut she knew exactly how he felt.

"Me, too," she admitted, locking her hands behind his eck and kissing him again.

His hands slid slightly under her shirt, skimming the ottom of her rib cage. When she had the wicked thought at she wanted him to go further, to keep going until he ached her breasts, she realized that the kiss had already iraled out of control.

"Jason. Jason, wait—mmm. No, wait! What if someone es us? What if *Emily* sees us?"

Immediately, he glanced over his shoulder, toward the ouse. Despite their being at the far end of the yard, they ould still be visible from the windows. They were in ain-enough sight to provoke questions like, "Hey, what's mily's dad doing to Aunt Ronnie?"

Since she wanted to avoid that, she pushed him away. ith great reluctance.

His arms fell to his sides, and he bent forward slightl
as though he'd just finished a series of wind sprints. "Do
this mean I misread you before? I thought you weren
sure about us…"

"Unsure about me," she clarified. "And Emily. She's i
credibly special, but kids are a huge commitment. Yo
must know that more than anyone. I didn't feel ready, b
I'm so close to…" *Falling in love with you.*

"So what changed your mind?" He searched her eye
"About being ready?"

If she admitted that she still felt semi-uncertain abo
her capabilities as an instant mommy, would she see
wishy-washy? A tease, seducing him out here again
the fence posts when she still had some conflicti
emotions? Or would he understand that getting involv
with him—and by extension his daughter—was a b
step and Ronnie cared too much for both of them to tal
it lightly?

"I'm still trying to sort it all out," she told him honest
"But I think…I think I'd rather sort it out with you than apar

"I can live with that." His smile was tender. "All I ne
for now is the promise that you're thinking about it."

An easily made promise—it seemed she'd been thinki
of little else lately. Then he kissed her again, and for
blissful few minutes, she couldn't think at all.

JASON DRAPED AN ARM ACROSS his daughter's shoulde
studying her sleepy, contented expression by the glow
a teddy bear lamp. Today had been a good day, for both
them. He glanced down at the book in his lap.

"You sure you want to hear *Three Billy Goats Gruff*

had never been a particular favorite, but she'd asked for
it nearly every night this week.

"Yes!" Emily nodded emphatically.

"All right." So he zipped through the story, doing the
voices that made her squeal with delighted laughter, then
set the book aside, knowing it was time to stop postponing
the announcement. "I have something I want to show you."

"'Kay," she murmured agreeably.

He reached to the nightstand, picking up a framed
picture he'd set facedown while Emily brushed her teeth
for bed. "You know who everyone in this photo is?"

She picked him out first. "Daddy!"

"Yep. And this cute baby I'm holding is you."

"Not a baby," she protested indignantly.

"Of course not, you're a big girl. But you started out as
a baby. Do you know who this other person is, on the other
side of me?"

She looked blank, and he felt bad for Isobel. Knowing
her daughter couldn't pick her out of a snapshot would
probably devastate her.

"This was your mother. Is your mother. She doesn't live
with us, but what if she could visit us?"

"When?" She didn't sound as instantaneously excited
as he'd predicted; rather she sounded a bit trepidatious.

"For your birthday."

"For my birthday wish?"

"Ah, not exactly. She loves you and misses you and
wants to see you soon, but she still can't live with us."

"Why not?"

And *this* was why he'd stalled having the conversation.
"Well...a lot of mommies and daddies live together

because they're married, because they love each other
Your mother and I got divorced."

This earned him nothing more than a puzzled stare.

"We…fell out of love with each other." That, at least
sounded better than saying Isobel couldn't handle motherhood.

Emily's lower lip trembled. "Will you fall out of love
with *me?*"

"No! Never." He hugged her tight. "It's different with
grown-ups. I know it's hard to understand, but your mother
and I both love you. Very much. And we both want to
share your special day with you."

"And Ronnie?"

"She'll be here, too."

Emily yawned. "Do you love Ronnie?"

Yes. The immediate answer, though he didn't voice it, was
a revelation. He'd known his feelings for her were strong, but
after today, watching her grapple with her fears and deciding
that Jason and Emily were worth facing them down…

"I care about Ronnie very, very much."

"So you'll kiss her?"

He simply grinned. *Whenever possible.*

RONNIE HADN'T EVEN PRESSED the bell yet when she heard
the doorknob being jiggled. A moment later, the door
opened. Both Jason and Emily smiled out at her.

"She's been watching through the front window for
guests," he said.

Ronnie stepped inside, bending down to wish Emily
happy birthday. "What a pretty party dress. Did your daddy
help you pick that out?"

Emily shook her head, scrunching up her nose as though he idea of her dad's fashion sense was already something he found preposterous. "Miss Wanda."

"Wanda was here earlier, to deliver the cake and help ie balloons on the back porch. She went to get Zoë just a minute ago."

Emily eyed the purple-wrapped rectangular box in the rook of Ronnie's arm. "That for me?"

"Nah." Ronnie winked. "It's for your daddy."

Emily laughed, obviously not fooled. Ronnie glanced p to see Jason watching them with a look of fierce joy n his face.

She rose, her eyes locked on his. "You're staring."

"Yes, I am," he said, giving her a thorough once-over. You look fantastic."

She smoothed her denim skirt just to give her hands omething to do. "Glad you approve."

When the doorbell sounded behind her, she turned, au- ɔmatically reaching for the handle because she was so lose. She opened the door to reveal an absolutely tunning woman, who shared Emily's dark hair and facial atures. *Isobel.* This was the woman who'd once shared ason's life?

She was wearing a linen tunic and slacks in the same erulean, looking incredibly chic for a child's birthday arty and also incredibly nervous. "Am I early?"

Ronnie cast a glance over her shoulder, not feeling ualified to answer on Jason's behalf.

"Your timing is fine."

Feeling like an intruder on a major family moment, onnie moved aside, bobbing her head in what she hoped passed for a greeting. This was the first time she'd been inside Jason's place and it registered distantly that the interior spoke more of a little old lady than the house's current owner. A small antique table just inside the door was covered with a yellowed doily and mail; a framed Bless This Home was cross-stitched in mauve and hung on the wall among baby pictures. Most of the photos were of Emily, but there were a couple of black and-white shots of a young boy and a color picture of a bald baby with Jason's eyes. Another time, those pictures might have made her smile. Now they seemed like reminders that he had a lot of history she didn't know, some of which had been shared with the woman standing in the foyer.

Jason knelt beside his daughter. "Emily, this is Isobel. Your mother. Can you say hi?"

It was hard to say which adult was the most surprised when Emily shrank back and hid behind Ronnie's legs, her death grip around the knees threatening to topple Ronnie. Isobel's eyes shimmered with tears, and Ronnie had the urge to apologize, although she couldn't fault Emily for being nervous. Jason escorted Isobel inside, and the woman trembled but kept her voice light and soothing.

"Hi, baby." The woman leaned forward but stopped suddenly when Emily made an anxious sound in her throat. "God, you're so beautiful. My beautiful baby girl."

At that, Emily straightened indignantly. "Not a baby."

A small laugh escaped Isobel. "No, of course not. It's been a long time since I've been here, but it still looks the same."

"You knew Gran-Gran?" Emily asked, curiosity winning out against bashfulness.

"A long time ago," Isobel said.

Jason cleared his throat. "I've got plans to redecorate, ut... Isobel, this is Veronica Carter."

"Nice to meet you," Ronnie offered. She'd like herself etter if she meant it more. The truth was, it was too easy) picture the effortlessly feminine brunette, her pint-ize daughter and Jason as the family they should have een. Which left Ronnie disoriented and feeling like a aird—fourth?—wheel.

Besides, even though he'd been divorced at the time and tonnie had been well within her rights, she felt uncomfort-ble now, standing in front of his once-wife with the knowl-dge that she'd slept with Isobel's former husband.

"I know the balloons are all taken care of," Ronnie said, but is there something else I can do to help while you aree...catch up? Or, I could stay and play hostess. Answer he door and stuff." That might allow them a moment's rivacy in the living room, time to adjust to each other's ompany before they were together under the scrutiny of iends and neighbors.

Jason shot her a grateful smile. "Emily, what if we show our mo—show Isobel your room?"

Then they were gone, leaving Ronnie alone with a arobbing ache. She pressed a hand to her chest, then her aidsection, but she couldn't locate the source of the pain r get it to stop. This was ridiculous. *She* had no reason to e frazzled when she should be doing a better job of sup-orting Jason and Emily.

A knock at the door caused her to jump, and she dmitted Zoë and Wanda Spencer, the Cline boy and his aother coming up the sidewalk behind them. After that, everyone arrived quickly. As Kaitlyn passed inside, she mouthed, *Is she here yet?*

Ronnie gave a barely perceptible nod, noting that it had been some time and none of the McDeeres had reappeared. When Emily did lead the way onto the back porch, she beamed at the pile of presents that had accumulated in her absence. Her parents followed, and there was a moment of awkward silence.

Jason greeted the guests with a jovial smile of welcome. "Hi, everyone! We're so glad you could join us for Emily's third birthday. This is Isobel Hawkins." He went through individual introductions, then turned to his daughter. "Well, princess, what game do you want to play first?"

But the birthday girl seemed too overwhelmed to respond. Ashley, by default of being the oldest and most outspoken, subtly took control, and Jason seemed happy to have direction, no matter who it came from. Soon, the kids were playing, and Ronnie's soul sang to hear Emily's deep laugh across the yard. After a few minutes, Emily ran to Isobel to share something amusing with her.

Ronnie's breath caught. *She's getting what she wanted for her birthday.* A mother. How many times in life did second chances like this really happen? How many times in her own life had she wished for five more minutes with her mom?

Gradually, the other adults warmed up to Isobel, complimenting her outfit or expressing interest in her "glamorous" symphony job.

Isobel turned to Jason. "Does Emily like music? Bang pot lids together or dance?"

There was such wistfulness in the woman's voice, and Ronnie felt a tug of sympathy for all the things Isobel

lidn't know about her own flesh and blood. A lump rose
n her throat. When she couldn't swallow it back, she
grabbed the nearly empty lemonade pitcher and hurried
nside, on the pretext of refilling it.

Once alone in the kitchen, she gripped the edge of the
counter and leaned over, her breathing harsh. She'd been
hinking a lot about happy endings lately. Wasn't *this* the
happy ending—a broken family given the chance to be
whole again? She and Jason were nebulous and undefined,
having only agreed to "think about" the possibilities. On the
other hand, he'd once exchanged binding vows with the
woman on the back porch, the woman who knew she wanted
to come back and be Emily's mother. Ronnie thought back
to those painful first moments when Emily wouldn't let go
of her leg and had only peered at her mother from beneath
the hem of Ronnie's skirt. *I'd get in the way.* She'd hamper
the mother-daughter bonding Emily had so wanted.

When she heard the back door open, she whirled
around, instantly relieved to see Kaitlyn.

"You okay?" her sister-in-law asked.

"Absolutely. Just getting more lemonade."

Kaitlyn raised her eyebrows at the still-empty pitcher.
"She's prettier than I expected."

"Why wouldn't you think she was pretty?"

"Well, I mean, there's *pretty,* and then there's yikes,
don't look directly at her or you'll be blinded by her
radiance. Still, looks aren't everything."

"She's trying really hard," Ronnie said. "That counts
for a lot."

"True, but if I had to pick between her or you—"

"It's not a competition!" Hastily, Ronnie refilled the

pitcher and headed back to the yard where she wouldn't
have to answer difficult questions.

The party mood had clearly been established. Jason was
spinning the kids around and pointing them toward a large
pink-and-purple piñata. Ronnie envied them the opportunity to bash the heck out of something. While the children
were occupied, Wanda set up the impressive castle-shaped
birthday cake Ronnie would never in a million years be
able to duplicate.

"I can't believe you made that," she said in awe.

Wanda winked at her. "If it makes you feel better, I
don't know how to change the oil in my car."

Isobel leaned forward. "So you're a mechanic?"

Ronnie nodded, explaining haltingly that she'd followed
in her dad's footsteps. This gave Adele Coombs the
opening to ask about Isobel's "people" and Ronnie learned
that Isobel's parents had had her late in life and lived in a
nursing home.

"I don't see them as often as I should, but the last time I
visited, it seemed to agitate Mom, the confusion of figuring
out who I was." Her laugh was brittle. "I'm sorry. That was
hardly cheerful party conversation, was it? How about I go
inside and get ice cream to go along with the cake?"

Ronnie squeezed her eyes shut, vowing never to take her
family for granted again. One would think that, after the
loss of her mother, she'd overlook any petty annoyances
her brothers caused and relish the simple gift of life, but
that kind of realization was difficult to sustain in the face
of daily tribulations. So she bitched about Danny's over-
protectiveness and rolled her eyes at Dev and forgot sometimes just how lucky she was.

Who did Isobel have? She was about to uproot to a new city, away from her current colleagues and friends, all in the hopes of setting right a single past mistake. Ronnie felt like a traitor. She cared about Jason and Emily; as such, shouldn't she be indignant and wary on their behalf? Wondering just how the hell a woman could have not appreciated them? Instead, she found herself admiring Isobel's courage.

Ronnie just hoped *she* had the courage to do the right thing.

Chapter Fourteen

By the time the party came to a close, the parents looked more in need of naps than the children. Ronnie certainly felt exhausted, emotionally drained enough to sleep for a week.

Kaitlyn squeezed Jason's arm as she said goodbye. "It was the social hit of the season." Then she hugged Ronnie, whispering, "Call me if you need to talk."

Soon, it was down to Jason, Isobel and Ronnie. And Emily grinning in frantic joy. She'd raked in a great haul of toys and now wanted all four of them to play together.

"I can't, Emily." Ronnie scooped the girl up for a hug and noisy raspberry on her cheek. "I should be going. Maybe another time?"

Jason took a step closer. "I'll walk you to your car."

She reflexively took a step away. "N-no, that's all right. I'm sure you'd like to rest. Nice meeting you, Isobel."

If Ronnie didn't literally sprint to her car, she was at least speed-walking. But if she was going to walk away from Jason, she needed to do it fast and put far more distance between them this time.

JASON TIPTOED OUT OF HIS daughter's room. She'd gone from hyperactive, post-party-frenzy to nearly comatose in a matter of moments. Recognizing the signs, he'd popped in a favorite princess DVD to lure her into lying down on the couch. She'd been asleep before the opening credits finished, and he'd carried her to bed so that he and Isobel could talk without fear of waking her.

Isobel was sitting at the kitchen table, looking up at him with something akin to the hero worship he remembered. Those glances that had called to him to *take care of me, love me,* and he'd been only too willing to do so. In the early days of their marriage her emotional fragility had seemed more flattering than burdensome. He wondered now if he'd loved the way she made him feel about himself as much as he'd loved her.

They'd both grown since then.

"That was amazing." She rose from her chair and came toward him. "Thank you so much. I can't tell you how much I'll treasure this day." She threw her arms around him in an exuberant hug.

He patted her back a bit clumsily. "It meant a lot to Emily, too."

Isobel pulled back, regarding him solemnly. "And you? Did it mean anything to you, the two of us together like old times?"

They'd never *had* old times like this, a shared family event. There'd been the two of them alone in their marriage, and then a wailing infant and equally weepy wife, both of whom he'd tried to comfort while balancing his own job and the household responsibilities. He tried not to resent her for that, liked to think he'd done his damnedest to be supportive, but he really had no desire to revisit those particular times.

He extracted himself from the remains of her embrace. "Emily will probably sleep for an hour or two. If you want to go back to the bed-and-breakfast, maybe we could meet you in town somewhere for dinner?"

She wrinkled her nose but somehow managed to make even that look elegant. "It's a small town where everyone knows you. Everyone was very nice today, but their curiosity was palpable. I'd feel like I was on display if we were out. Why don't we just order in? I have some possible ideas for redecorating this place if you're looking for suggestions."

He bristled. "You can't walk into a house for the first time in five years and start handing out tips on how to decorate it!"

"Sorry." She ducked her head. "Of course you're right. It's just…that's the kind of thing I know how to do and I was trying to find a way to help. To repay—"

"You don't owe me anything," he assured her, feeling churlish for his outburst. "It was a clinical condition you suffered from. I don't blame you."

Her expression brightened. "You mean that? Because there's nothing I'd like more than a fresh start. You were the best thing that ever happened to me, Jace. Even through the divorce proceedings, I never stopped thinking of you. Either of you. But I honestly thought my being gone would be better for you both. It's not too late to pick up the pieces, is it? I know it would take time, but I can be patient, if you'll just tell me you're willing to consider it."

The words were eerily similar to what he'd told Ronnie yesterday, that he didn't need anything from her but a promise to think about it. Now unease stole through him. He'd been thinking in terms of giving Isobel a second chance with her daughter. Did she think they could recapture the romantic elements of their marriage together as well?

"Are you suggesting that you and I—"

"Well, not right away, of course. I abused your trust, and, frankly, we've both changed. I thought…maybe we could give dating a try?"

"Dating?" He didn't want to laugh at her, he could see she was earnest. But he couldn't help seeing a kind of absurdity in the situation. Principal Schonrock wanted him to date, Caren Hanover was trying to set him up with women, now here sat his ex-wife calmly proposing he date her. "Isobel, the truth is, there's someone else I already have feelings for."

She swallowed. "I see. I suppose it was too much to hope for, but when you didn't seem to have a girlfriend…"

"She's not, exactly. The truth is, we don't know what we are." *But we were hoping to find out.*

"Oh, but then, if you're not committed to her, maybe we could still go out, find out if—"

"Isobel. Please don't." It was awkward enough rejecting her; he didn't relish the thought of standing here and doing it repeatedly.

"All right." She stood, giving him a sad smile. "I should leave, then."

"The house," he clarified. "Or town?"

"For now, just the house. Eventually, I'll have to leave town, too, but I plan to come back if you and Emily will have me. My running-away days are behind me."

Well—he recalled Ronnie's hasty exit—that made one woman in his life who planned to stick. What about the other one?

WHEN RONNIE DROVE AROUND the garage to park in the small employee back lot, she saw that Jason was already there. She winced. He'd called and left two messages yesterday that she hadn't returned. She planned to tell him she'd worked herself into exhaustion in her yard, taken a shower and gone to bed early.

All true.

Of course, she'd stared at the ceiling, unable to sleep into the wee hours, but he didn't need to know that. He was sitting on the hood of his parked car, cradling a cup of coffee. She could see little tendrils of steam rising above his hands. More alarmingly, she fancied she could almost see steam coming out of his ears. Was he angry that she'd dodged his call? Or that she hadn't stuck around yesterday?

Her father's car and Danny's were both parked in their usual spaces. If she got Jason to come inside with her, where there was an audience, would the conversation remain calmer, or would she just end up having to explain a lot to her eavesdropping family afterward? She took a deep breath, mentally girded her loins and approached him with a tentative smile.

"Good morning."

He quirked a brow. "That remains to be seen."

His tone was a definite change. He'd always been such a gentleman, encouraging her to give them a try but exhibiting understanding and compassion when she'd had her doubts.

"Are you angry?" she asked bluntly. Might as well find out for sure rather than pussyfoot around.

"I think I'm just bracing myself for a difficult conversation."

Difficult? Maybe she could let him off the hook, make this easier for him. She took a deep breath. "Jason, if you've come to tell me that we shouldn't see each other, I understand."

Judging from the immediate glint of metallic anger in his eyes, that had been the wrong thing to say.

"No, dammit, that is not why I wanted to talk to you!" Okay, now he was unmistakably angry. "Were you hoping I would, so that it would save you the trip?"

Yes. "Don't you sneer at me, this is a complicated situation, and I'm trying to do the best I can." She knew that every person had their own emotional baggage—Lord knows she had her share—but with Jason, there was so much that she expected to see a bellboy following him around town. It had been difficult enough to wrap her mind around Emily, who was young and trusting and charming, without bringing the beautiful and sympathetic ex-wife into the mix.

Jason's expression softened as he slid off the car. "Doing the best you can...that's something I can relate to. And I probably get it wrong a lot. For instance, I *probably* should have started the conversation with this: I love you, Veronica."

She gasped. *He loved her?* "I…"

"Love me, too?" He smiled boyishly. "Because I cannot tell you how much that would make my day."

She wanted to smile back but sobered. "What about your wife?"

"My very ex wife. There's nothing romantic between us anymore."

"Are you sure?" she pressed, thinking again of the rarity of their situation, the chance to heal Emily's family. "You don't strike me as a man who takes the emotion lightly, and you once loved her enough to pledge the rest of your life to her. Don't you owe it to yourself—"

"You promised that you'd at least think about it," he reminded her. "About us. Yet you're seizing the first excuse handed you to dismiss it."

What? She struggled with her temper, wanting to penetrate the frustration he radiated so she could make him understand. "If Isobel hadn't suffered that depression, wouldn't you still be with her now? I grew up missing my mother, but Emily doesn't have to! I'm trying to do the right thing by at least giving you the chance."

His eyes narrowed. "The right thing, or the easy thing?"

"That's not fair!" He was being cruel and she would have despised him for it if it weren't so clear his words were coming from a place of pain. Pain *she* was causing him.

· "You're talking to the wrong guy about fair." He gave her a sardonic smile. "I seem cursed to fall for women who easily walk away from me at a moment's notice."

Seeing the slump of his shoulders made her ache for him. She reached out a hand, but he jerked away before she could touch him.

She was tempted to apologize, but she wasn't sorry for trying to give him the necessary time and space to at least think the situation through.

"I told Isobel that our marriage is over. If she can accept it, can't you? When she walked out, I blamed myself, trying to figure out ways I could have fought harder to hold us together. But the truth is, Ronnie, a relationship takes two people. I couldn't make her stay then, and I'll be damned if I'm going to grovel for you to stay with me now if you don't want it enough." With quiet dignity, he added, "I deserve better than that."

And then he was gone.

BY WEDNESDAY, RONNIE WAS going crazy at work. After her family's initial questioning, "What's wrong?" and her rather manic insistence that she was fine, they'd stopped asking. Yet they treated her gingerly, as though navigating a minefield. It was annoying to be so emotionally on edge, making her feel extra "girlie" compared to her brothers, bringing to life all the stereotypes about women being weepier or more sensitive.

Well, I'm not! She'd barely cried over Jason at all.

Although, in her weaker moments in the middle of the night, she'd let herself replay his declaration in her mind: I love you, Veronica. It had been so tempting to reach for him and say the same. Wouldn't that have been the selfish reaction, taking what she wanted? Wasn't she doing the unselfish thing by removing herself from an emotionally fraught situation so that Jason and Emily and Isobel could work on repairing fractured relationships?

She wished it was as easy to understand people as it was cars. She worked well past normal closing hours, needing the rhythm of the garage, the step-by-step procedures that calmed her nerves. Her father and Danny had both left for the day, so she started when she heard footsteps.

"Hello?"

"Just me, Red." He handed her a cold can of soda. "Why

don't you take five, come hang out with your much cooler older brother for a few minutes?"

She smirked. "Whatever you say, Devin *Eugene*." He'd always been the one brother who, no matter what her mood, stood the best chance of making her laugh.

He took their father's chair since he could prop his feet up on the desk—Danny's desk was far too crowded for that. "As a guy, I know I'm not all that tuned to other people's feelings, but give over. Something's obviously upset you. Lola Ann says you won't even confide in her. We're both worried about you."

It was weird to think of them as a united front. Ronnie took a sip of the soda. Talking about Jason was like picking at a painful scab, but *not* talking about him all week hadn't made her feel any better.

"He said he was in love with me," she said softly.

Devin's eyebrows shot up, but for a moment he said nothing. Then he kicked his feet off the desk and sat straight. "The *bastard*. How dare he?"

She wanted to crack a smile, but her facial muscles wouldn't quite comply. "Dev, this is serious."

"We've noticed. What I don't get is why you aren't, you know, happy."

"I'm trying to do the right thing. I let him go."

"Being noble is overrated."

"Devin! Quit making jokes." She stood, squeezing the can.

"Sorry." He stood, too, hugging her from behind. "Sorry I warned Lola Ann that she'd be better at talking to you than I would."

"It's nice you two are finally together," Ronnie said, wondering how serious they were but kind of afraid to ask

"Well, I resisted it, but I think you've got my stubborn streak beat by a mile."

It wasn't stubbornness…it was fear. Outside of the garage, Ronnie had felt inadequate at so many things. If someone made a wish list of what qualities a good mom or wife needed, how many of them would she have? She didn't want to disappoint Jason and Emily, not after everything they'd been through.

"What if I'm not enough?" Ronnie asked. "What if I tell him I love him, too, and down the line, he regrets not taking the chance with the woman he really loves?"

"Sounds to me like you *are* the woman he really loves."

"He married a porcelain-skinned cellist with fine arts degrees and classical training. You saw her, she looks like a goddess." It would be hard for Ronnie to top that even if she *could* cook a decent meal without burning anything or sew a child's Halloween costume, the way their mother had handmade Ronnie's when she was little. *I can't create those memories for Emily.*

"Ronnie, do you trust me?" Devin asked.

She snorted. "Trust the guy who once tricked me into 'snipe hunting' and left me in a dark forest? Hell, no."

He chuckled at the adolescent memory. "Good times. But we're adults now and I might actually have decent advice. You've accused us of running off guys, and, fine, that was true sometimes, but do not run off the one guy I've seen make you truly happy. You're going to have to take the plunge."

"And if it doesn't work out?" she asked, still hoping for that guarantee even though she knew better.

"Then at least you know you tried. Life's short. Make the most of it, Red."

On some level, she knew he was right. It was why she'd avoided talking to everyone, because she was afraid Kaitlyn or Lola Ann would give her advice she wasn't ready to hear.

She punched his arm. "You're surprisingly deep, you know that?"

"Tell no one."

She grinned, feeling cautiously happy for the first time since leaving Jason's house. "Who'd believe me?"

Chapter Fifteen

Jason headed to his car Thursday afternoon, reminding himself that, as of next Monday, Nina would start baby-sitting again. With Wanda Spencer helping him tomorrow, today should be the last time he had to pick up his daughter at Kaitlyn's house. It wasn't that he didn't appreciate her help over the past couple of weeks—she was a very nice lady—but he didn't need any more reminders of Ronnie than the ones his mind already provided twenty-four/seven.

Maybe he'd simply pushed too hard, implying an ultimatum that she had to love him back. Arrogant, in retrospect, except that he'd been so sure… His relationship with Ronnie was so different from his marriage that he'd been excited by the possibilities, moved by how great she was with his daughter and aroused by the woman herself.

Damn. He flipped on a blinker. He was doing it again, getting lost in thoughts about her. Well, no more. How difficult could it be to move on from a woman he'd only been involved with for a short while?

He hadn't even turned off the street where the high school was when his cell phone rang. "Hello?"

"Hey, Jason. It's Kaitlyn. Can't really talk right now, but—"

"Is everything okay?"

"Yeah, no worries. Just, there's been a…troop emergency. And I'm troop mom, so… I just wanted to let you know that Ronnie has Emily at her house. You can pick her up there. Bye!"

She didn't give him the chance to ask questions before hanging up. What constituted a troop emergency? Her entire rushed explanation had been bizarre. And so much for his plans not to think about Ronnie.

He tried to look on the bright side—this gave him the chance to be civil. He'd been highly irritated with her the other day, and she shouldn't have to bear the brunt of his previously failed relationship. It only took him a few minutes to reach her house; he didn't feel prepared to go knock on her door and face her again. However, since she had his daughter, there wasn't much choice.

A sticky note on the door read Bell Works. He pressed the button and sure enough heard chimes throughout the house. Ronnie opened the door, wearing—oddly—her mechanic's coveralls.

"I understand you were nice enough to take my daughter in. Again."

She bit her bottom lip. "Not exactly. More like I wheedled and cajoled and bullied Kaitlyn into letting Emily spend the day with me. Please don't be mad."

He was more confused than angry. "Where is she?"

"Helping me set the table for an early dinner. I was hoping you'd stay."

"Look, Ronnie, I don't—"

"Please." She took his hand, and a zing went through him.

What the hell was going on? He recognized the look in her eyes, but tamped down his heart's inclination toward hope. He didn't want to be disappointed again.

"I cooked," she said.

There was something funny about the way she said it, but, then, this whole situation was funny. He followed her into the kitchen and scooped Emily into a hug.

"Did you have a good day, sweet pea?"

The girl nodded, then launched into an exuberant recitation of events. He could only follow every second or third word but gathered that she'd been assigned the important task of handing Ronnie instruments from the toolbox *and* she'd been allowed to help make dinner.

"Emily, can you go in the other room and watch that movie I cued up for you?" Ronnie asked. "I want to talk to your Daddy, okay?"

"Okay." She giggled and looked at Jason.

He was beginning to feel that everyone was conspiring against him. Once his daughter had skipped out of the room, he looked expectantly to Ronnie.

She was stirring something at the stove. Then she placed the lid back on a pot and came to sit with him at the table. "I wanted to borrow Emily today because I wanted to get to know her even more, get to know myself *with* her. I should tell you, I'm not very good at saying no."

He thought of all the times he'd let Emily stay in his room instead of carrying her back to her own despite the advice of Wanda Spencer and his mother. "I'm not perfect in that area myself, but I try."

She let out a breath. "I tried, too, to put you out of my

mind when I was afraid I wouldn't be right for Emily, for you. But I failed miserably."

That spark of hope flared again, but he waited for her to continue.

"Thank you for telling me that you loved me. It was one of the best moments of my life—which quickly turned into one of the worst because I was afraid to say it back. I really thought that maybe you and Isobel… Jason, I love you, too."

Joy seized him, stealing his breath, as though there wasn't any room inside him for anything but her. She obviously had more to say, but he pulled her into his lap, kissing her. He eyed the zipper at the top of her neck-to-ankle coveralls.

"Are you wearing anything under that?" He'd never seen all the true fantasy potential of a mechanic's uniform until now.

Laughter burbled out of her. "Even if I said no, there's not much we could do about it now." She jerked her head toward the other room.

"Not that I'm complaining, but why are you dressed like that?"

"Well, I don't have a washer and dryer… No, actually, I wanted you to see me for who I am. I know I dressed up for our date to the Spring Fling, but it took three friends to advise me on the outfit. Half of the time, I look like this."

He ran his gaze over her. "You look pretty good to me."

"When I iron, I somehow put as many creases into the material as I get out. I can fix a doorbell and change a tire, but I'm one really, really bad cook."

"Ronnie, what are you talking about?"

She pulled away from him. "Here, let me show you." Taking him by the hand, she led him to the stove and handed him a spoon. "Beef Stroganoff, my mother's recipe."

To humor her, he took a bite, even though he didn't see what— "Oh! Oh, that's, um…"

She gave him a pitying smile. "Want to order a pizza?"

"Yeah, could we please?"

"I'm not perfect," she said. "You were right the other day. You *do* deserve better."

"No. I was angry, but that's not how I meant it." He tugged her closer, smoothing her hair away from her face, looking into the green eyes that were a turbulent sea of vulnerability. "Before you have a baby, you do all this preparation, trying to make the right home for them—putting together a nursery, all kinds of weird plastic baby-proofing. When we brought Emily back from the hospital, things were strained from day one. Isobel barely even wanted to hold Em. Then after Isobel left, it just felt weird to be there. Wrong.

"I've bounced around and nothing ever felt like home, although Gran's was the closest I've come. But even though I've done the major stuff, reinforcing beams and securing light fixtures to keep the place safe for Em, I've dawdled on everything else. I never picked out a color scheme to redo my bedroom, never chose new curtains or wallpaper. I tell myself it's because I'm busy, but… I think it's also because the place doesn't truly feel like my home. Ronnie, when I'm with you, for the first time, I feel home. You make me comfortable and happy and I don't give a damn how bad your beef Stroganoff is. I love you."

Happy tears had started to run down her cheeks, and she

sniffled. "That's the sweetest thing anyone has ever said to me. So, what do we do now?"

He kissed the side of her neck, up toward her earlobe. "We order pizza, ask Emily if she wants to have a special sleepover at your house, then I make love to you as quietly and thoroughly as possible."

She shivered with need. "That sounds like a good plan. But, beyond tonight? We're probably going to have to make some tough decisions, adjust to some major changes. Overcome some doubts."

He paused, studying her face and catching one teardrop on his thumb. "You still have doubts?"

"More like insecurities," she admitted. "But they're not nearly as strong as what I feel for you and Emily."

The little girl must have gotten bored with her movie and curious about what the adults were up to, because as soon as Ronnie said her name, she rushed toward them.

"I wanna hug, too!"

Her father laughingly obliged, scooping her into the center of the embrace so that the three of them could hug.

Emily squirmed around to face Ronnie. "Are you gonna be my mommy?"

Jason shot Ronnie an apologetic glance, then admonished his daughter, "Let's take it one day at a time."

But that night, as Emily drifted toward sleep on a palette made specially for her, Ronnie leaned down to kiss her good-night and whispered, "I'd love to be your mommy."

It was the first of many mother-daughter secrets and a lifetime of joy.

Enjoy a sneak preview of
MATCHMAKING WITH A MISSION
by B.J. Daniels,
part of the **WHITEHORSE, MONTANA** *miniseries.*
Available from Harlequin Intrigue
in April 2008.

Nate Dempsey has returned to Whitehorse to uncover the truth about his past...

Nate sensed someone watching the house and looked out in surprise to see a woman astride a paint horse just on the other side of the fence. He quickly stepped back from the filthy second-floor window, although he doubted she could have seen him. Only a little of the June sun pierced the dirty glass to glow on the dust-coated floor at his feet as he waited a few heartbeats before he looked out again.

The place was so isolated he hadn't expected to see another soul. Like the front yard, the dirt road was waist-high with weeds. When he'd broken the lock on the back door, he'd had to kick aside a pile of rotten leaves that had blown in from last fall.

As he sneaked a look, he saw that she was still there, staring at the house in a way that unnerved him. He shielded his eyes from the glare of the sun off the dirty window and studied her, taking in her head of long blond hair that feathered out in the breeze from under her Western straw hat.

She wore a tan canvas jacket, jeans and boots. But it was

the way she sat astride the brown-and-white horse tha
nudged the memory.

He felt a chill as he realized he'd seen her before. In tha
very spot. She'd been just a kid then. A kid on a pretty pain
horse. Not this one—the markings were different. Anyway
it couldn't have been the same horse, considering the las
time he had seen her was more than twenty years ago
That horse would be dead by now.   .

His mind argued it probably wasn't even the same girl
But he knew better. It was the way she sat the horse, so a
home in a saddle and secure in her world on the other side
of that fence.

To the boy he'd been, she and her horse had representec
freedom, a freedom he'd known he would never have—
even after he escaped this house.

Nate saw her shift in the saddle, and for a moment he
feared she planned to dismount and come toward the
house. With Ellis Harper in his grave, there would be little
to keep her away.

To his relief, she reined her horse around and rode back
the way she'd come.

As he watched her ride away, he thought about the way
she'd stared at the house—today and years ago. While the
smartest thing she could do was to stay clear of this house
he had a feeling she'd be back.

Finding out her name should prove easy, since he figurec
she must live close by. As for her interest in Harper House..
He would just have to make sure it didn't become a problem

* * * * *

Be sure to look for
MATCHMAKING WITH A MISSION
and other suspenseful Harlequin Intrigue stories,
available in April
wherever books are sold.

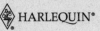
HARLEQUIN®

INTRIGUE

WHITEHORSE MONTANA

No matter how much Nate Dempsey's past haunted
him, McKenna Bailey couldn't keep him off her mind.
He'd returned to town to bury his troubled youth—
but she wouldn't stop pursuing him until he was
working on the ranch by her side.

Look for

MATCHMAKING WITH A MISSION

BY

B.J. DANIELS

*Available in April
wherever books are sold.*

HI693

HARLEQUIN

More Than Words

"Autism—a national
health crisis.
Get informed.
Get involved. I am."

—**Curtiss Ann Matlock,** author

Curtiss Ann wrote "A Place in This World," inspired by Dr. Ricki Robinsor
Through her practice and her work with **Autism Speaks,** *Dr. Ricki has*
provided hope to countless parents and children coping with autism.

Look for "*A Place in This World*" in
More Than Words, Vol. 4,
available in April 2008 at eHarlequin.com
or wherever books are sold.

HARLEQUIN

SUPPORTING CAUSES OF CONCERN TO WOMEN
WWW.HARLEQUINMORETHANWORDS.COM

MTW07RO

REQUEST YOUR FREE BOOKS!

2 FREE NOVELS PLUS 2
FREE GIFTS!

American ★ Romance®

Heart, Home & Happiness!

YES! Please send me 2 FREE Harlequin American Romance® novels and my FREE gifts (gifts are worth about $10). After receiving them, if I don't wish to receiv any more books, I can return the shipping statement marked "cancel." If I don't cance I will receive 4 brand-new novels every month and be billed just $4.24 per book the U.S. or $4.99 per book in Canada, plus 25¢ shipping and handling per boc and applicable taxes, if any*. That's a savings of close to 15% off the cover price understand that accepting the 2 free books and gifts places me under no obligatic to buy anything. I can always return a shipment and cancel at any time. Even i never buy another book from Harlequin, the two free books and gifts are mine keep forever.

154 HDN EEZK 354 HDN EE.

Name _____ (PLEASE PRINT)

Address _____ Apt. #

City _____ State/Prov. _____ Zip/Postal Code

Signature (if under 18, a parent or guardian must sign)

Mail to the **Harlequin Reader Service:**
IN U.S.A.: P.O. Box 1867, Buffalo, NY 14240-1867
IN CANADA: P.O. Box 609, Fort Erie, Ontario L2A 5X3

Not valid to current subscribers of Harlequin American Romance books.

Want to try two free books from another line?
Call 1-800-873-8635 or visit www.morefreebooks.com.

* Terms and prices subject to change without notice. N.Y. residents add applicable sales ta Canadian residents will be charged applicable provincial taxes and GST. This offer is limited one order per household. All orders subject to approval. Credit or debit balances in a custome account(s) may be offset by any other outstanding balance owed by or to the customer. Plea allow 4 to 6 weeks for delivery. Offer available while quantities last.

Your Privacy: Harlequin is committed to protecting your privacy. Our Privac Policy is available online at www.eHarlequin.com or upon request from the Reade Service. From time to time we make our lists of customers available to reputabl third parties who may have a product or service of interest to you. If you would prefer we not share your name and address, please check here. ☐

H

The Taken

Tierney Doyle is used to being criticized for
her psychic abilities, yet the tough-as-nails—
and drop-dead-gorgeous—detective has no doubt
about what she has uncovered in the case of a
string of unsolved murders. And Tierney is slowly
discovering that working so close to her partner,
detective Wade Callahan, could be lethal.

Look for

Danger Signals
by Kathleen Creighton

Available in April wherever books are sold.

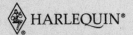

HARLEQUIN®

American ★ Romance®

COMING NEXT MONTH

#1205 RUNAWAY COWBOY by Judy Christenberry
The Lazy L Ranch
Jessica Ledbetter has worked too hard on her family's dude ranch to let
Jim Bradford, a cowboy turned power broker and the ranch's new manager,
show her up. The Lazy L is Jess's legacy, and she isn't about to let it fall into
the hands of an outsider. No matter what those hands can do to her...

#1206 MARRYING THE BOSS by Megan Kelly
When Mark Collins finds himself in a competition with Leanne Fairbanks for
the position of CEO of the family business, he can't believe it. But as they go
head-to-head in a series of tasks to fight for the top job, Mark begins to see her
as more than just a rival. And if he wins, will he lose *her?*

#1207 THE MARRIAGE RECIPE by Michele Dunaway
Catching her fiancé in bed with one of the restaurant's curvaceous employees
sends up-and-coming pastry chef Rachel Palladia fleeing Manhattan for the
comforts of home. But when her ex threatens to sue for her dessert recipes, she
turns to her high school heartthrob, Colin Morris, who happens to be the town
lawyer—and he's a lot sweeter than revenge!

#1208 DOWN HOME DIXIE by Pamela Browning
No real Southern belle would fall for a Yankee—especially not one named
Kyle Sherman. But Dixie Lee Smith does, and hides the truth about his
illustrious ancestor from her family. What's worse, as soon as she finds out
she's got competition, *she* goes to war—to keep the handsome Northerner
for herself!

www.eHarlequin.com

HARCNMM0